Ride Clear of Daranga

The town was locked up tight. Hired killers made it unhealthy to ask questions and most people rode clear of Daranga. But three Justice Department men had died violently in the Rio Blanco country and the attorney general wanted the men responsible.

He had a surefire way of cleaning out cesspools like Daranga: send Frank Angel. Here was a gun artist, swift, deadly and merciless. If anyone could bring law and order to the town it would be Frank!

Ride Clear of Daranga

Daniel Rockfern

A Black Horse Western

ROBERT HALE · LONDON

ISBN-10: 0-7090-7646-0
ISBN-13: 978-0-7090-7646-9

Robert Hale Limited
Clerkenwell House
Clerkenwell Green
London EC1R 0HT

Typeset by
Derek Doyle & Associates, Shaw Heath.
Printed and bound in Great Britain by
Antony Rowe Limited, Wiltshire

CHAPTER ONE

When they come at you out of the darkness, there is perhaps one second to make the choice: kill them or run. MacIntyre was a good man, trained to think fast, but he wasn't expecting trouble and so he made the wrong decision. The two men were professionals and good at their job and they had the advantage of surprise. They left him huddled dead in an alleyway on the north side of town and moved away silently into the night without arousing a flicker of interest from the passers-by on the brightly lit street a few yards away.

Two days later Mike Stevens was efficiently knifed outside a cantina in San Patricio. Two miners going in for a drink saw the scuffle and ran into the street as they saw Stevens fall. His throat was slit and the blood was still pumping in a red arc from his jugular vein long after the sound of hoofbeats faded into the night. Somebody said later that there had been two men, one of them tall and dark haired.

Inside the same week someone discovered what was left of Oliver Freeman. He was staked out in a patch of prickly pear, his eyelids cut off the way the desert Apaches used to do it, and smeared with molasses to attract the ravenous red ants. He had been out there a while, and they had to bury him on the spot because nobody would bring his body into town.

CHAPTER TWO

The Attorney General's office was a high-ceilinged, spacious room on the first floor of the huge building which housed the Department of Justice. Outside it stood two armed Marines flanking the big, brass-studded, leather-covered doors. One of them opened the doors now for the Attorney General's private personal secretary, Miss Rowe. A tall girl, with honey-colored hair falling loosely about an oval face, her blue eyes were impish as she said to the visitor:

'He's expecting you.'

'Ma'am,' said the man.

Amabel Rowe regarded him speculatively. Tall, rangy, his broad shoulders straining the seams of the dark grey suit, Frank Angel had the look of far horizons in his eyes. Amabel Rowe knew that he was a Special Investigator for the Department; this was by no means his first visit to this office. From time to time she had seen letters and reports from him mailed in godforsaken spots out West: Texas, Indian Territory, once even Oregon. She had also seen his terse reports at the end of his assignments and knew that the man smiling as he went past her into the big sunlit office was a killer.

The Attorney General rose and came around the desk to meet his visitor, his hand outstretched.

'Frank, I'm glad to see you! he exclaimed. 'How's that arm?'

'Good as new now,' Angel said. 'Little stiffness for a while, but it wore off. I got plenty of exercise down at the range.'

The Attorney General nodded. 'Sit down, sit down,' he said, motioning to a chair, and proffered a box which contained some very long dark cigars. Angel grinned and shook his head.

'I'll stick to tobacco if you don't mind, sir,' he said. 'The last time I smoked one of those things it took three days for my voice to get back to normal.'

The Attorney General sniffed, and selected one of the evil-looking cigars from the box, lighting it and puffing on it, inhaling the noxious smoke with every evidence of huge enjoyment. He let the smoke drift from his nostrils in a long, slow, luxurious exhalation.

'Aaaah,' said the Attorney General. 'Wife won't let me smoke these in the house – damned interferin' woman. Still, that's neither here not there. Now, Frank . . .'

Angel leaned forward infinitesimally in his chair.

'You've been briefed?'

'Prosser down in Records was very thorough,' Angel told him. 'Showed me the reports on MacIntyre and Freeman. Wasn't much on Stevens.'

'And your conclusions?'

'Hard to say,' Angel replied. 'Freeman, now. That could've been some drunken buck off the Reservation. It isn't likely, but it's possible. Whoever did kill Freeman had the soul of a Chiricahua, if not the blood.'

The Attorney General nodded. 'And so?'

'So – no coincidence.'

Again the man behind the desk nodded. Angel waited until the cigar was relit and then the Attorney General leaned forward, hands clasped.

'I sent them all out there, Frank. All looking for different bits of the same puzzle.'

'You think they were on to anything?'

'No, I think they were killed to make sure they didn't get on to anything.'

Angel leaned back in the armchair. 'Better fill me in,' he said.

'OK,' the Attorney General said. 'We had a few scattered reports of thieving at first. Nothing much – just a line in the US marshal's reports that ranchers in the Daranga area were complaining about rustling. Then another report, this time from the Indian agent at San Simon. He told us he was being offered cattle well below market price, as many as he wanted. He had to buy them; on the allocations he gets for his Apaches, every dollar counts. But he mentioned it, and I added that information to the fact that two men named Birch and Reynolds were buying every piece of land in the Rio Blanco country that they could lay hands on, and every piece of property they could get into. They purchased the franchise for the post tradership at Fort Daranga, and we got one or two complaints that they were charging monopoly prices for goods. When people tried to go someplace else, they found the market controlled for a hundred miles around by these same two men. They pretty well bought up Daranga – the hotel, the general store, built a fancy saloon, started living it up like feudal barons. None of which was in itself illegal, but it made me curious. I sent MacIntyre to Baranquilla to check on the land office records there. Stevens was checking up on some men we'd heard were supplying stolen beef to Birch and Reynolds. Freeman was scouting the country, asking questions.'

'And they all turned up dead,' Angel mused. 'Interesting.'

'*Interesting* is hardly the word,' was the harsh reply. 'Frank, I'm worried. I have the uneasy feeling that something big is brewing down there, and whoever is behind it has access to knowledge about this Department. I can't put a finger on it, but I smell something and I want to know what it is.'

'Three of our men dead is enough,' Angel said gently.

'Damned right it is!' snapped the Attorney General, slapping his desk with the flat of his hand. 'I want you to get out there and snoop around. Find out what's going on. It stinks of politics, and I want to know who and I want to know why, Frank.'

'All right,' Angel said. 'I'll get started tomorrow.'

'Draw two hundred dollars as expenses,' the Attorney General said. 'You can account for it when you get back.'

'If I don't come back do I get to keep the money?' grinned Angel. His remark brought a grim smile to the face of the man opposite him.

'That's not such a hell of a joke, boy,' he said. 'There's someone out in that country who's quite willing to kill without warning or mercy to protect whatever scheme he's concocted.

8

Tread softly, play it carefully.'

Angel nodded, his face sober.

'How will you travel?'

'I'd say Missouri Pacific to Trinidad,' Angel said. 'I can head down the Rio Grande to Las Cruces and across into Arizona from there. Be in Daranga about a week from now.'

'Good,' the Attorney General said, rising abruptly. 'Take good care of yourself.' His face was set and unsmiling.

'Always do,' Angel replied. He didn't smile either.

CHAPTER THREE

'Well, hoss, Satan sure made a fine job of it,' Angel observed to the indifferent animal as he hauled on the reins. The dun tossed its head impatiently, wanting to get on down off the crest of the ridge where the midday heat blasted down like a tangible force.

'Know we're near water, that it?' Angel grinned. 'Probably you can smell those Army hosses, too. Well, you can hold on five minutes longer.'

He hooked a leg around the pommel of the saddle and surveyed the country rolling out below the ridge, checking its physical proportions against the knowledge acquired by long study of every map the Topographical Department had been able to show him.

Below and stretching away as far as the eye could see lay a sunblasted wilderness in which nothing moved but the shimmering heat haze, a wilderness of rock and sand and slow-rising sandstone mountains and dry flats of searing white alkali. Across it ran a thin trail that looked like a whitened vein; away to the southeast lay Daranga City. Swinging his body to the right, Angel let his eyes follow the trail to where it forked. There lay the Army post, Fort Daranga, from which the town some forty miles away had taken its name. It looked like all

Army posts: galleried officers' quarters, the long low line of bunkhouses, stables, quartermasters, saddlers and other buildings all set four-square around a graveled parade ground that blazed chalkwhite in the sun, a flagpole smack in its center. Angel figured that the Army had a model somewhere that they copied, regardless of the location. Thus they were able to make certain that the officers and men froze in the winter and fried in the summer no matter whether the fort itself was in the high Rockies or out in Apache desert. He shrugged; only fools and failures needed uniforms, anyway.

He spurred the horse into motion, and the dun snorted gratefully, picking its way carefully down the faint trace. Angel had cut across the corner of Dobbs Butte, coming into the country the way a careful man would come – wary of main roads, wary of settled places, keeping just that few miles off the beaten path that meant safety for the rider of the long trails. Angel himself was dressed in ordinary range clothes. He was glad to be out of the city, and already the sun had burned back the saddle leather brownness of his skin. He no longer realized that his eyes were restless, always watching the country he was riding through, the habit of a decade that he was no longer even aware he had. His life had been a mixture of this one and of good living in the East, and he looked upon those periods now realistically as rewards for performing the tasks the Attorney General set for him. The money was good and he enjoyed what it could buy in Manhattan or Washington or New Orleans. The dangers he faced were a fair price to pay: he wished neither to be rich nor old. He had no desire to end his days a drooling old nuisance in a wheelchair. And he had seen the rich in the almost innumerable empty forms they came in. The only thing you could do with money was spend it. To keep it was a sickness, and to want it for its own sake worse than cancer. He moved on down the trace now, a big, wide-shouldered man, a bandolier of ammunition around his shoulders, the high sun picking cruel highlights off the metal cartridges and the weapon at his hip.

He dismounted outside the sutler's store, a big building

with a Dutch barn roof that stood catty-cornered on the north-eastern side of the fort. On its timber face was painted the legend *Reynolds & Birch, Merchants*. He pushed in through the screen door and went inside, his spurs clinking on the rough board floor, pausing a moment to let his eyes adjust to the cool dark interior. It was a big L-shaped room. Merchandise of every kind was on display, on the counters, in boxes on the floor, hanging from the walls: whiskey and beer bottles glinted on shelves, the dull gleam of leather: saddles, belts, bridles, glowed richly. Flat brown boxes of cartridges, nails, screws. Cans of biscuits, dried fruit, cans and boxes in profusion. It was a well-stocked store and he figured that the owners must have a good business to be able to carry such a wide range of goods. At the far end of the building a rough zinc bar was backed by shelves on which stood an assortment of bottles and kegs. A few soldiers were sitting around a table, deep in conversation that ceased as they looked up to eye Angel speculatively as he walked across to the bar. They measured him carefully, accurately judging his origins and probable occupation, eyes pausing momentarily on the low-slung gun and the bandolier of cartridges; then they returned to their muted conversation. An elderly man in buckskins slouched against the bar. Further down, two men, half hidden in the cool shadows, gazed blankly at the wall, drinks cradled in their hands. Angel nodded at the bartender, a short, sweating, baldheaded man with a pronounced limp.

'I'll take the longest, coldest beer you've got,' he said.

'Beer,' nodded the bartender. 'Comin' up.'

The glass was full and frothy, the beer sweet and cool. Angel pushed the glass forward.

'And again,' he said.

'OK,' said the bartender. He swabbed down the bar, looking for some way of opening a conversation. Angel made it easy on him.

'Good beer,' he said.

'The best.'

'You ship it in from the East?'

11

'Nope. Got our own brewery up in the hills, 'bout two miles from here.'

'That so? That's unusual, isn't it?'

'These sojer boys'd drink us out on paydays,' the bartender explained. 'If'n we didn't have our own supply, we'd be out o' beer six days from seven.'

'Yeah, I see what you mean. This is sure some store you got here.'

'We do all right,' the man said. 'Where you headin'?'

'Daranga,' Angel told him. 'How far is that from here?'

'Forty mile, give or take.' A pause, with more swabbing of the bar that was as dry as it would ever be. 'Passin' through?'

'Depends,' Angel said, not reacting to the prying tone. 'If I can find me something to do, I might stick around. Any of the local spreads lookin' for men?'

'Well . . . I couldn't rightly say, mister—uh. . . ?'

Angel ignored the invitation to provide his name.

'What you're sayin' is, it depends on what kind of men, right?'

The bartender ducked his head and scowled, swabbing furiously at his scarred bar counter.

'I never said that,' he mumbled. 'I ain't no information bureau.' He started to move away.

'Hold it,' Angel said softly. There was nothing in his voice which made the words remotely threatening but the bartender stopped in his tracks, his eyes wide.

'Now lissen, mister . . .' he began.

'You couldn't mebbe give me one or two names so I could ask in Daranga, could you?' Angel said. 'Not wantin' to give you any unnecessary trouble, I mean.'

One of the soldiers got to his feet. He was more than half drunk and it took him a moment to focus his eyes properly on Angel. He walked unsteadily across the room, ignoring the muttered objections of his companions. He put his hand on the bar and faced Angel owlishly.

'Cowboy,' he said, carefully enunciating the words, 'take the advice of an old soldier and keep right on past Daranga.'

12

Angel smiled, and motioned to the bartender to fill his glass again.

'I see you're a soldier,' he said easily. The boy might not take offense but he had no desire to antagonize him by an unfortunate phrase, 'but I'd hardly say you were old. Will you take a drink?'

'I am, nevertheless, old,' said the boy, nodding sagely, 'and I most definitely will. Take a drink. Yes.'

'You were sayin' about Daranga. . . ?' Angel prompted.

'Your health, sir. Daranga. Yes. Give it a miss, cowboy. The town is owned, as we are owned, by Mr Birch. Rich Mr Birch. Powerful Mr Birch. Nobody works in Daranga unless he says so. Nobody can buy a drink unless it's his liquor. Nobody can broil a steak unless he bought it from Birch. An' Reynolds, o' course. Good ol' Jacey Reynolds.' He put the glass down on the bar with a bang. 'I'd buy you a drink, sir, but I regret to say that I am already in debt to this establishment to the tune of two months' pay.'

Angel grinned, and motioned to the bartender to fill up the glasses. The man was sweating very badly and kept darting glances at the two men down at the far end of the bar. They were still looking straight ahead, as if the room were quite empty. The man in buckskins had slipped out of the place as quietly as a mouse. Angel felt the tension and did not for the moment identify its source.

'Thank you, kind barkeeper,' said the soldier. 'I drink to your health, sir.' He lurched slightly. 'Steady, Blackstone. I drink to the health of my fellow-officers and, ah, gentlemen. I drink to the health of Mr Birch. And his sidekick Mr Reynolds. And to their iron fists and thieving habits . . .'

One of the other soldiers got up and came across to Blackstone, putting an arm around his shoulders. 'Come on, Blackie,' he said, 'knock that off. Excuse him, mister,' he said with a pleading glance at Angel and then at the two men along the bar, who were still ignoring the proceedings, 'he's just plain drunk. He'll be all right when he's had a slee—'

Blackstone threw off the friendly arm. He looked indignant,

13

but it was the indignation of the drunk who knows he is wrong and does not care.

'Drunk, is it,' he said. 'Well, maybe. Ain't so drunk as I can't tell a man the truth. Any man!' he said defiantly, glaring at the indifferent duo along the bar. 'Take my advice, stranger. Steer clear of Daranga.'

'Blackie—' remonstrated the other soldier. 'He don't need your advice. And we don't need no trouble with Al Birch, neither.'

Blackie again shook off the restraining hands.

'No. Lemme alone,' he said deliberately. 'S'about time someone said it. Tol' truth. Owns this place. Owns the whole goddam place. Not a man here isn't up to his ears in debt to them for liquor or women or cards or some damn thing. When he says shit everybody better squat, and you can tie to that.'

'I'll keep it in mind,' Angel said. 'You'd better—'

Without warning he was thrust aside by a burly arm, and the two men who had been studiously ignoring the conversation went on past him and confronted the young soldier.

'You're doin' a lot o' jawin', Blackie,' one of them rasped.

'Huh? Oh, h'lo, Johnny.'

'Don't hello me, you little bastard,' snapped the one called Johnny. 'I've warned you before about the way you shoot your mouth off.'

'That's right,' whispered the second man. Angel really looked at him for the first time. Short, squat, the man had in his eyes a look which was identical to that of a rattler eyeing an especially juicy prairie dog. His tongue flickered out and touched wet, full lips. His right hand, covered in a fine black kid glove, clenched and unclenched. Angel had never seen a man in this country with such white skin. The man's fat face showed no sign that the sun had ever touched it. He was dressed in brown: brown shirt, brown leather pants that stretched skin tight across his enormous back and buttocks. He lisped slightly on the letter 's' when he spoke.

'That's right,' he repeated. 'You know Al doesn't like it, Blackie. And that means we don't like it, either.'

'Birch is a first-class sonofabitch, Mill. You know it and I know it and everyone else knows it. Stopping people sayin' it won't change the facts.'

Blackie was erect and his eyes flashed with anger, but those watching knew that the alcohol was doing a lot of the talking. There was a great silence in the room.

'You keep callin' Birch names, you're liable to wind up in the desert, face-up with the buzzards pickin' on you,' grated the one called Johnny. He was a man of medium height; his hair was long and streaked with grey, and he wore the vest and pants of a blue serge suit. His shirt was almost white and had figured patterns stitched into it. He wore no tie or kerchief around his neck, and his hat was a wide brimmed derby, slanted to one side of his square head. His eyes were set deep in his head, and huge dark pouches were etched beneath them. His face was high-cheekboned and drawn, and Angel recalled seeing such faces in hospitals back East. It was the face of a man dying of a pulmonary disease. The thin shoulders and bony physique reinforced the similarity.

Angel eased his weight onto the balls of his feet as the boy stepped back slightly from Johnny, his eyes widening at the venom in the man's words.

'Now just hold on there a minute, Boot. This is an Army post, not some one-horse cowtown saloon. I'll say what I please.' Just for a moment the boy's eyes flickered towards his friends, who sat frozen at their table.

'You'll say you're sorry,' whispered Mill, 'or you'll bite on a bullet.' The two men moved apart slightly, both of them keeping their eyes on the soldier. The other soldier, the one who had tried to calm Blackstone down, moved away, his jaw dropping slightly and his eyes wide with fearful anticipation.

'Now see here, Johnny,' he began.

'Quiet,' whispered Mill. 'You're ruining my concentration.'

One of the men at the table shoved back his chair and leaped towards the door, determination on his face. 'Corporal of the guard!' he yelled, 'Corp—' With a lithe bound amazing for one of his bulk, Miller was across the room and beside the striding soldier, his gun moving in a blur from holster to hand and up and down, falling with vicious certainty. The soldier fell as if hit with an ax, his leg twitching momentarily. A trickle of blood oozed from his right ear.

Blackstone gazed at the fallen man in horror. The drunkenness had fallen from him like a cloak, and he realized in his cold sobriety that the two men before him were in a killing mood, a flat and unemotional mental state which would be all the more ferocious for its coldbloodedness. His eyes moved wildly to right and left, his thoughts as plain as if they had been printed on his forehead. High noon, officers asleep, enlisted men dozing, the nominal guard playing cards in the orderly room, no one likely to stir for another hour or even two. He had to face it alone. His chin came up.

'It'll take the two of you,' he said calmly.

'Lovely,' said Mill. The two men advanced on the boy, who retreated backwards until he was brought up short by the bar behind him. At that moment, Boot slapped the boy across the face. The sound had the shocking suddenness of a pistol shot in the silent room and for a moment, Blackstone stood frozen with disbelief, the red welts of the older man's fingers imprinted clearly on his beardless face. Then a strangled scream of fury burst from his lips and he threw himself forward, clawed hands reaching for Boot's neck. Boot grinned like a cat and dropped his shoulder slightly, moving it upwards to meet the oncoming face. The soldier ran into the shoulder, rock hard, braced expertly to meet his charge. It stopped him dead in his tracks and he reeled off to the side, blood bursting from his lips and nose, down on his knees and mewling through the smashed mouth. As he scrabbled to regain his feet, Mill, lips wet with anticipation, drew back his spurred and booted foot, ready to deliver a rib-breaking kick to the unprotected body of the boy. There was an angelic smile on his face. He and Johnny had done this many times. He always enjoyed it.

'Ah, no,' said Angel, who was moving even as the boy sprawled to the scarred board floor. With a smooth and powerful movement he caught Mill's foot from behind, fingers curling around the instep. He jerked upwards and back, stepping away easily as Mill went face forward into the floor, smashing himself hard, blood and dust and dirt smearing together on his broken face, half unconscious from the impact, his head almost touching the feet of Johnny Boot, who whirled around, his hand flashing for the sixgun holstered at his right thigh.

'Now that'd sure be stupid,' Angel said mildly, freezing Boot to the spot.

The muzzle of Angel's gun was steady, and pointed directly at his middle. From a range of three feet, no man could miss, and Johnny Boot knew better than most what a .45 bullet in the stomach could do. His lips went back from his teeth and he let his weight settle on his heels. Mill got up from the floor, spitting, furiously pawing sawdust and blood from his face.

'By God,' he hissed. 'You'll pay for this.'

'Don't ruin your day waiting for it,' Angel said coldly. 'Put your hands on the bar where I can see them. Move.'

He lifted Mill's gun out of the holster, followed suit with Boot's, and handed them to the gaping bartender.

'Stay neutral, friend,' he said to the man. 'Put these somewhere out of reach – theirs and yours.'

The bartender nodded hastily, almost eagerly. He hurried to do Angel's bidding, then stood away from the trio and watched them, hypnotized by the events.

Boot had now regained control of himself. He turned warily from the bar, hands well in view, and hooked a heel on the rail.

'Mister,' he said conversationally, 'I wonder if you know what you've got yourself into?'

'Looked like as nasty a whipsawing as I ever saw,' Angel said. 'I just naturally felt I had to butt in.'

'Teachin' a young pup manners,' snapped Boot. 'None o' your business.'

'You're a stranger here,' whispered Mill. His face was puffing badly and his piggy eyes looked even more evil. 'You're starting out purty bad.'

'Tell me,' Angel smiled. The gun muzzle remained level

and unwavering.

'Put your gun away, stranger,' Boot said. 'Fight's finished.'

'Really?' said Angel, letting the sixgun slide easily into the holster.

'Sure thing,' said Boot flatly. 'You're small beer, mister. We ain't got no need to beat up on drifters, no matter how mistook they are.' His voice took on a tone that was almost wheedling. 'Al Birch is the top man around these parts. It's no boast: he is. He is because we keep him that way. We're what you might call his major suppliers. Now you could buck us, an' you might even get away with it. But you can't buck Birch, stranger. Don't even think about it. Get on your horse, point him back the way you come, an' never come back. Sabe?'

'I reckon,' Angel nodded.

'Good.' Boot's smile was the smile of a wolf seeing a calf leave the herd.

'I'll tell you what me and Willie are goin' to do. We're goin' to step outside for a couple of minutes. That'll give you time to have a beer and be on your way. Don't be here when we get back.'

Angel nodded. 'One last thing,' he said mildly.

Boot turned to face Angel again, his face resigned and his bearing that of a man reasoning with a stubborn child. 'What now?' he barked.

'This,' Angel said. His arm was moving even as he spoke and all his weight was behind the perfectly timed punch that came up from somewhere around his hip and took Boot clean on the point of his jaw, lifting him perhaps an inch off the ground and sending him cartwheeling backwards against the wall. Boot smashed into the solid adobe with a crash that shook the building, and everyone heard the dull clunk of sound when his head hit the brickwork. He went down on the floor like a dropped sack.

Angel turned to Mill. His tone was still conversational.

'Why don't you give your friend a hand? I don't think he's going to make it home on his own.'

Mill looked at Angel for a long moment. There was something furtive and sick in his piggy eyes. He said something beneath his breath.

'Physiologically impossible,' Angel said cheerfully, 'although it's sure imaginative. Maybe I should break enough of your bones to see if it can be done.' The bantering tone dropped from his voice and he took a step towards Mill, who cringed backwards, fear – and something else – showing in his eyes. Angel shook his head.

'Get out of here, Mill,' he said. 'You're contaminating the air. Take that' – he pointed at Boot's still form – 'with you.' He took another step forward and Mill scuttled back, heaving at Johnny Boot's body. One of the soldiers stepped forward to help and Mill rebuked the man with a vicious curse. He wrestled the unconscious body towards the door, sweat streaming through the bloody dust on his face. Never once did he look again at Angel.

CHAPTER FOUR

The news of the fracas spread like wildfire around the Fort. It was not long before the sutler's store was crowded with people, with all ranks of men from the Fort, all eager to see the man who had finally given Boot and Mill the bad time every man there wished them. A bearded old Irishman who chewed tobacco and spat with engaging ferocity and alarming accuracy, came into the store with a battered medical bag and proceeded to clean up the young officer's face, managing through the entire time not to breathe one question about the cause of his injuries. Finally, he could contain himself no further.

'Dadblast it, Blackie,' he exploded. 'Must I die of curiosity before ye'll speak?' His voice had a rich green brogue.

Blackstone managed to look surprised. 'I thought everyone knew by now, Doc,' he said.

'Aye, lad, I daresay they do,' grinned the old doctor, rattling a spittoon some twenty feet away with a jet of tobacco juice. 'But 'tis the details we're longing for. The lovely, juicy details.'

The onlookers crowded around again as Blackstone proceeded to tell in ever-exaggerated detail, exactly what had happened to him and then what had happened to Mill and Boot. When he finished, there was a shout of delight, and everyone looked around for the man who had effected this small miracle. He was nowhere to be seen.

'Hold on, now, hold on,' Blackstone told them. 'I'll go and see where he is.' He went out into the sunshine, and after he had asked two or three men around the parade ground, came upon a sergeant who had seen someone answering Angel's description heading for the stables. Blackstone went into the pungent-smelling, muggy building. He found Angel grooming the ragged coat of the lineback dun he had ridden in on.

'You ran out on us,' Blackstone said, breathlessly. 'I figured to at least buy you a drink.'

'Another time, maybe,' Angel said. 'I'm not much on cheering crowds.'

'Me neither,' agreed the youngster. 'Mister, I owe you. An' I don't even know your name.'

'Angel, Frank Angel.'

'Frank. My name's Richard Blackstone.'

'How long you been out here, Richard?'

'Goin' on two years. Why?'

'Nothin' special,' Angel said. 'Just like to hear you tell about the conditions in these parts.'

'Well . . . gladly,' Blackstone told him. 'But look: won't you at least let me try to repay you in some way? Would you – would you be my guest for dinner? It's bachelor grub, I'm afraid, but you'd be very welcome. An' I think I have a bottle of wine we could split between us.' The boy blurted out the words as if afraid that by stopping he would give Angel an opportunity to refuse. A slow grin crossed the older man's face.

'Why, that would be very pleasant, Richard,' he said. 'I'd be happy to do that.' Blackstone's face broadened into a boyish –

if lopsided – grin.

'Why, you can stay overnight if you've a mind,' he said. 'My friend Jamie Kitson is away on leave in Kansas City, so I have our quarters to myself.'

'He the same rank as you?'

Blackstone nodded proudly. 'We joined the service the same day.'

'Lieutenants,' Angel said shaking his head. 'They get younger every year.'

Blackstone grinned at the old joke. He turned and headed for the doorway, stopping to face Angel before going out.

'Seven o'clock, right after retreat suit you?'

'Down to the ground,' Angel assured him. 'I'll be there.'

When he finished caring for the horse, Angel walked around the Fort. He noted the thick outer walls of the perimeter buildings, the sloping roofs and the forest of chimneys on each. The officers' quarters ran across the best side of the Fort, that was to say the side which would receive the least of the sun – northeast to southwest. He noted the positions of the commissary and the dispensary, the CO's house, the adjutant's office, the guardroom and the jail. There were five rows of enlisted men's barracks on the opposite side of the square to officers' row. The flag hung limp on the tall sapling pole in the center of the parade ground. He saw one or two tame Apaches, not many. Right now, the Army and the Apache were at peace. The Fort wore an indolent air. Discipline slack? He had read the record of its commanding officer, Brevet Lt. Colonel Brian Stuart Thompson. He knew, in general, the man's background and the campaigns in which he had fought. It had been an unspectacular career, and marred by indiscretions. Drinking had brought about one specific black mark which had ensured that Thompson would never rise above his present rank: there had been a General Court Martial and allegations of adultery with the wife of another officer at Fort Griffin. The charges had been unproved, but the black mark had remained. Thompson had friends in Washington but even they were not powerful enough to have the records whitewashed. He would stay on frontier posts like this one until his retirement.

He found the row of adobe huts that housed the laundry-women, wives of enlisted men or their common law women, and paid one of them a dollar to heat him a tub of water. After the bath in a big old washing tub, he changed into a clean shirt and Levis and found a cool spot beneath a ramada to watch the ageless ceremony of retreat, savoring the sweet sad sounds of the bugle. Then he ground out his cigarette and walked across to Blackstone's quarters.

Blackstone met him with a warm smile and showed him proudly around the cramped rooms which were his home. The furniture was sparse and makeshift: a wooden chest of drawers, two armchairs and a stuffed sofa that had somehow found its way to the Fort. The floor was of packed dirt and the walls limed adobe. Indian blankets had been hung on them to add a splash of color, and Blackstone's dress sword hung crossed on its scabbard above the fireplace. The table was neatly laid for two. An orderly served them a decent meal of boiled meat and boiled potatoes, canned fruit and fresh bread from the post bakery. The wine was pleasant and light, although far from cold. Afterwards Blackstone produced some cigars and a bottle of whiskey. He poured a generous measure and watched expectantly as Angel sampled it.

'Jesus!' Angel said. 'Where did you get that?'

'A patrol took it off some traders. Probably on their way to sell it to the Indians,' the boy said.

Angel shook his head, blinking the tears from his eyes. 'That's the real stuff,' he coughed. 'All of ten minutes old.'

They went out on to the cool porch behind the house and put their feet up on the porch rail. Angel led the conversation towards Mill and Boot.

'They play rough,' he observed. 'What's their racket?'

'Cattle,' Blackstone told him. 'They steal them.'

'You know that for a fact?'

'No, of course not,' the young soldier told him. 'But it's the local talk. Johnny Boot got out of Texas two jumps ahead of the

Rangers a few years ago. Mill with him. They'd been thieving there, cutting cattle out of herds an' driving them into New Mexico to sell on the Mescalero Reservation. The prices they asked, nobody had too many questions.'

'And here?'

'Same thing,' Blackstone explained. 'Birch an' Reynolds have the beef contract for the Hot Springs Apaches. There are a few other ranchers around here: George Perry an' Big Walt Clare over to the north-east. They say they're losing cattle all the time. Birch an' Reynolds never do. Folks around here say they've got a miracle herd. No matter how many head they sell to the Army or the Indians, they always have the same number of head left.'

Angel nodded, encouraging the boy to continue.

'Of course, the Army tends to turn a blind eye. First, rustling is a civil matter, not a military one. If a man comes along with unbranded beef an' offers it at a price the others can't compete with, that's not the Army's problem. The Army's problem is to feed the Indians as cheap as possible.'

'What about the agent at Hot Springs?' Angel asked.

'They say he's part of the ring,' Blackstone said. 'Not out loud, of course.'

'Boot and Mill again?'

'Yeah. Johnny Boot is a killer. They say he's very fast with the gun. And Mill – well, you saw him. I think he's sort of half crazy . . . likes to see people beaten up. If he killed a man, it'd be slowly.' Blackstone shivered a little, though the night was still warm. 'Gives me the creeps thinking about it. Which is why I want to thank you again, Frank—'

'Richard, let's not get into all that again,' Angel said. 'Anybody'd have done the same.'

'Well, I owe you one, anyway,' said Blackstone. 'I won't forget.'

'So Birch and Reynolds just about control the business in these parts,' Angel prompted.

'Pretty much. They have a brewery up in the hills, about ten miles from here. Reynolds' Addition, it's called. There's gambling up there, and women. Half of the men on this Fort owe money to them.'

'And the town?'

'Off limits to us,' Blackstone said. 'They keep things pretty clean down in Daranga. Tame sheriff. There's only one place doesn't belong to them, and that's The Indian's. Mostly Mexes an' such go in there.'

They talked as the stars came startlingly alive in the black-blue heaven, millions of them, seemingly close enough to touch. A cool wind came in off the chaparral, and there was the soft scent of sagebrush. When they turned in, Angel had a pretty clear idea of the layout of the whole area, and thanked his luck that he had so early found someone who could fill him in on what to expect. Birch and Reynolds had the country in their hands. Bribery, extortion, even murder seemed to be part of their catalogue, and complete financial and physical control their aim. He nodded, turning over before sleep. The pattern was emerging.

CHAPTER FIVE

Angel was awake and dressed before reveille. He stood beneath the ramada savoring the cool sweetness of the morning air and watched in the yellow dawn as the enlisted men stumbled from their huts beyond the parade ground, heading for the latrines, stretching and scratching, grumbling good-naturedly at each other, their voices clear in the still half light. The stretching notes of the bugle spread sweet across the valley. He knew the routine of the day which would follow, like the routine of every other day. The drills and the exercising, the caring for the horses of the cavalrymen, the long easy siesta-like middle of the day with light lunches in the officers' mess. It was time to go.

Blackstone came hurrying out as the bugle call soared into silence. He was stuffing his shirt into his trousers, struggling with his uniform jacket at the same time.

'Damn,' he muttered. He loped towards the assembling ranks of men, suspenders dangling. Angel smiled. Some men loved the army.

He headed down towards the stables, saddling the dun without haste, filling his canteens at the pump, checking his rifle and pistol for dust, going carefully over the horse's hoofs. He was busily doing this when he heard the regular tramp of feet coming into the stable, and turned to see a young officer flanked by two enlisted men heading towards him. The young officer came to attention and saluted. The enlisted men stayed rigidly behind him.

'Mr Angel, sir?' Angel nodded. 'Colonel's compliments, sir, and would you step across to his office.'

The boy was looking through Angel's head into some far off place.

'He say why?' Angel asked mildly.

'No, sir,' the young man said.

'You his adjutant?'

'Yes, sir,' the officer said. 'Lieutenant Peter Ellis at your service, sir.'

'Thank you, Lieutenant Ellis. Will you tell the colonel I'll be over right away?'

The young man looked embarrassed and shifted his feet a little. His face started to get red.

'My orders were to accompany you, sir,' he said, still staring away on through Angel's head.

Angel frowned. 'You mean it's not a request, it's an order – right?'

'Sir,' Ellis said.

Angel shrugged. 'Let's get at it, then.'

'Thank you, sir,' Ellis said. At his command the two enlisted men fell in behind Angel. They marched across the parade ground, focus of all eyes. Angel realized that it would look to any bystander as if he was under arrest. He saw Richard Blackstone detach himself from one group and come hurrying across to intercept the little phalanx.

'Lieutenant Ellis!' Blackstone snapped. 'What is this?'

'Colonel's orders, sir.'

'This gentleman is my guest,' Blackstone said. 'Is he under arrest?'

'No, sir,' said Ellis, plainly uncomfortable.

'Then why—'

'Are you questioning my orders, Mr Blackstone?'

Angel looked around to see that a tall, well-built man of about fifty had come out on to the porch of the office towards which the squad had been heading, and stood now, feet apart, glowering at the group.

'Sir,' Blackstone stammered. 'I was just—'

'Kindly attend to your duties, sir,' snapped Thompson. 'Mr Ellis, be good enough to bring Mr Angel inside.' He turned on his heel and went into his office ignoring the sergeant who jumped to his feet behind the desk just inside the door.

Ellis dismissed the squad and extended an arm towards the open door of the colonel's office. 'If you please, sir,' he said. He came in behind Angel, and Thompson looked up from the papers he was examining.

'That will be all, Mr Ellis,' he said. Ellis saluted and turned on his heel, closing the door behind him. Angel stood as the colonel bent his attention on the papers again, frowning in concentration. After a few minutes, Thompson looked up.

'Now, then,' he said. 'Mr Angel.' He said it with a kind of satisfaction, as though he had been savoring the moment.

'You wanted to see me?' Angel asked.

'I have a report here' – Thompson shuffled the papers – 'that you were involved in an altercation yesterday in the sutler's store.'

Angel said nothing. It had not been a question.

'Have you anything to say, sir?' Thompson's voice was harsh, a cultivated harshness. It did not escape Angel's notice that the man's eyes were bloodshot, and his uniform already speckled with cigar ash. He had the slouch of a man who had spent many years unprofitably behind a desk, and the greedy mouth of someone who felt he deserved better things. The teeth clamped on the cheap-smelling cigar were yellow.

'I tried to prevent one of your men being tromped to death, if that's what you mean,' Angel replied.

'I see,' Thompson said. There was a sneer in his tone, as if he had already adjudged Angel's action and found it that of an interfering fool. 'You do admit that there was a brawl and that you were involved.'

'I just told you that,' Angel said. He kept his voice level.

'I am perturbed, Mr Angel,' Thompson said. He tapped his teeth with the stogie. 'It is bad enough to have brawls on a military post. To have brawls which involve civilians and military personnel is even worse. It leads to bad feeling between the civilian population and ourselves, Mr Angel. I do not care to have that happen.'

'You'd like it better if they killed one of your men?'

'You are impertinent, sir,' snapped Thompson. 'I am well able to take care of any disturbances which occur on this post.'

'I don't doubt it, Colonel,' Angel said reasonably. 'But there wasn't a hell of a lot of time to wait for help.'

'That, sir, is none of your concern,' ranted Thompson. 'I will not have my officers involved in brawls. Lieutenant Blackstone will be punished severely for his part in it. As for you, sir, I have not yet made up my mind.'

'Then let me make it up for you,' Angel said, a coldness coming into his voice which stilled the soldier's anger. 'There's only one thing you can do to me. You have the power to escort me to the boundaries of this post, and you have the power to bar me from entering again without your permission, and so informing your men. Now since I was just about to leave anyway, why don't we just be reasonable about it instead of all this performance to impress your men with what a tough old bastard you really are?'

Thompson had risen to his feet during Angel's speech, and his face had gone brick red. Angel watched the man as he fought to control himself, and saw the anger fade, leaving behind an evil smile that worked its way to the surface of the colonel's face.

'Sergeant!' called Thompson. The door burst open, and the grizzled old three-striper came into the room on the double.

'Sah!' he yelled.

'You will take four men and escort Mr Angel five miles beyond the perimeter. You will see that he speaks to no one. Do you understand? No one.'

'Sah!' The sergeant frowned.

'Enter my judgment accordingly in the roster, Sergeant,' Thompson said.

'Sah.' The soldier looked at Angel and jerked his head. 'On your way, boy.'

Angel swung on his heel and walked to the door. Thompson sat down and glared at his papers, looking up as Angel left the room.

'If he is seen here again – shoot him on sight!' he hissed.

'Sah.' The sergeant closed the door and straightened up. He shook his head.

'You're in big trouble, boy,' he said. His eyes were like holes in the sand. 'Wait here, and don't do nothin' stupid.'

He went outside and Angel heard him summoning a squad of men. Presently he was escorted out into the sunlight, where his horse was waiting. His gunbelt was looped around the pommel of the saddle. He swung into the hurricane deck, and reined his horse around.

'Don't make the mistake of layin' a hand on that gun, boy,' warned the old sergeant. He nodded towards his squad. Angel saw that two of the men had Spencer rifles across their laps, and the guns were cocked.

'No, sir,' Angel said. The sergeant led the way across the parade ground and troopers averted their eyes as the procession swung into single column ahead and jogged on to the dirt packed road. They headed west with the sun hard on their backs, moving steadily down the trail. There were deep shadows on the canyon walls of Dobbs Butte. The country was flat and harsh; ocatillo, prickly pear, mesquite, barrel cactus, cholla speckled the sandy waste. The Fort fell behind and then out of sight as they moved down a slight incline, the horses making a small dust cloud which lifted and fell behind them. After about fifteen minutes, the sergeant held up his hand and brought the column to a halt. He turned in the saddle.

'Bring him up front,' he ordered.

Angel's horse was led forward. The sergeant pointed off to the west.

'Yonder lies Tucson,' he said. 'About a hundred miles. North lies Baranquilla, but you wouldn't like it there. South is Daranga, which you'd like even less. Back behind is the Fort, an' if you turn up there we'll shoot your ass off. Any questions?'

Angel shook his head. 'Seems right clear to me,' he said.

'Git movin',' the sergeant told him.

'After you,' Angel said. The old soldier glowered at him.

'Move, I said.'

Angel shook his head. 'They tell me it's real hard to know whether a man's been shot trying to escape, or just plain shot,' he said. 'I don't want anyone worrying that way about me.'

'You think we'd backshoot you?' the sergeant asked. There was amazement in his voice. 'Soldiers?'

'It's been done,' Angel said. 'Even if it hadn't, I wouldn't want to be the first.'

The old sergeant leaned heavily forward in his saddle, pointing a gnarled finger at Angel.

'You,' he said, 'are very close to gettin' your brains beat out. Let me tell you something, mister. I've served in this man's Army for nigh on thirty years. I've served with good command-ing officers an' bad ones, an' I've learned one thing: no matter what I think about it, the CO is always right. Now I heerd about you an' young Blackie, an' personally, I'm delighted you beat the shit out of them two cow thieves. That's my personal point of view. But as a soldier I have an order. Right or wrong, I'm carryin' it out. No more, no less. Now git out of my sight, Mr Angel, 'fore I forget myself.'

'Sarge, I'm sorry,' Angel said. 'You got to admit this isn't what you'd call usual.'

'On your way, mister,' snapped the soldier. 'I ain't got all day to jaw.'

He slapped Angel's dun across the rump with his own reins and the startled animal jumped into a gallop, heading on down the incline towards the open malpais below. When Angel turned around, the squad was already kicking up dust on its way back to the Fort.

He eased the horse into a walk, letting his thoughts get into order. The soldiers had done what they were told, as the sergeant had said; right or wrong, their CO was their CO. But what was the point of Thompson's insistence on his being escorted from the post? The man knew that any self-respecting rider could turn his horse's head and find his way to wherever he wanted to go, and Thompson must know that he would turn towards Daranga. Yet he had obviously given specific orders to head Angel towards Tucson. He took a bearing on the mountains off to his left. He was about five miles from the Fort. Over the mountains, making easy time, he could be in Daranga tomorrow evening. The sun was climbing high now and he felt its heat on his shoulders. It would soon be too hot to travel. He lifted the sixgun and belt from the pommel and started to strap it on. As he did so, something caught his eye. He lifted the belt and examined it more closely. A curse escaped his lips. The shells in the belt had been removed, and empty shells substituted. A quick flip of the cartridge showed that the gun was also loaded with empties. He pulled the carbine from its saddle holster, worked the lever. An empty shell came up into the breech. He did not bother to check his saddle-bag. The extra cartridge bandolier would not be there. So he had been set up! How and for what, he had yet to learn. Another thought struck him, and he swirled the canteen looped on the saddlehorn. It was empty. So that was it! Cast adrift in the desert, without ammunition or water! If he turned towards the nearest source of aid, the Fort, he would be shot on sight at the colonel's orders. What had the old sergeant said? Tucson, a hundred miles west. Baranquilla to the north, but he wouldn't like it there. A warning that Baranquilla was also hostile country to him? And south, Daranga. Forty miles or more. By no means an impossibility, even without water.

Besides, there were ranches between him and there. The frown of concentration deepened between his eyes. Somewhere . . . his eyes flickered across the featureless waste ahead of him . . . somewhere out there someone was waiting, ready to ambush him, as soon as he came near the trap. And all Angel could do was to ride into it.

He kicked the horse into movement.

CHAPTER SIX

Angel rode south. He moved alone through the immensity of the wilderness, a tiny speck against the towering emptiness of the desert, quartering across a line drawn due south, looking for the bed of the river he knew must be somewhere in this area, a tributary of the Rio Blanco called the Ruidoso, the Noisy River. Ahead of him, etched purple and black against the sky, the Baranquillas tumbled up towards the white sky. Angel knew that when he got further south he would be able to see the three peaks that marked the cut between the twin ranges of the mountains, the river pass through which he could head southeast for Daranga, along the valley of the Blanco. He let the horse make its own pace. And always as he rode, the grey eyes moved restlessly, missing nothing. Jackrabbits hitch-kicked out of the mesquite ahead of the plodding horse as the animal picked its way around the cholla. Once the horse brushed its nose against one of the cactus plants, tossing and snorting as the spines pricked its tender skin. They called cholla jumping cactus: it seemed sometimes to leap across the space between an animal and itself, planting those deadly numbing spines in the skin. Kangaroo rats hopped panicked from his path. Once he saw a sidewinder, flat head low and seeking, moving in ungainly loops across a sandy open patch.

He watched especially for birds. Quail gobbled in the safety of sparse bushes, but he never saw them rise. Sweat ran down his forehead and into the collar of his shirt; his body was wet with it, then a moment later as dry as a bone as the sun leeched the moisture from his skin. He moved relentlessly on into the wilderness.

The sun moved over in its zenith, sliding slowly down towards its destiny in the west. 'Come on,' Angel muttered once. His lips were thick and caked with alkali. The horse's head was hanging low. Two days without water was as much as either of them could take, he thought. He pushed the tired animal up a slight rise and then from the higher ground he saw the dark line of trees about three or four miles away. The Ruidoso: that must be it! He shook the reins. The horse pricked up its ears as well.

'Could be, hoss,' Angel said. 'Could be.'

The animal moved more quickly, almost as if it could scent salvation. Lurching now and then, but moving more quickly, the man and the animal were conscious now that there might be water ahead. Even if the river were dry, Angel knew there would be enough water below the ground to keep him and the horse alive.

Almost an hour later, he headed the horse down a shelving bank into the arroyo which in the brief rainy season would carry the Ruidoso River. He almost fell from the saddle, scrabbling at the sand with his bare hands, cursing the stuff as it sifted through his fingers back into the shallow hole he was digging. The horse snorted once as he dug, but Angel ignored it, his whole mind focused on the task of getting down to where the water might be. He was so involved in his task that he did not hear them until the slight crack of a twig breaking behind him brought him up on his knees, whirling to face their attack, but in that moment they were on him and something slammed against his head and he went down, face forward on the sand. He was not unconscious, and he half rose to his knees again, his mind whirling with unformed thoughts, reaching for the blurred figure he could see before his face. Something smashed down on his forearm and he cried out in anguish as the arm went completely numb. Once again, something crashed against his head above the ear and he went hurtling down into an endless pit, spiraling, whirling, flutter-ing down like a leaf from some very tall tree, never reaching bottom where the ultimate blackness lay, some freak stubborn-ness keeping his mind still clawing for consciousness. There was no pain when he felt the boot grind his other arm, although he knew somewhere in his mind that he was being hurt. Although he did not know it, his body obeyed the frantic signals of his brain and he tried to get up, although he was out on his feet, and he heard, as from some far place, a rasping voice he seemed to recognize say: 'Kill the bastard.' Death was very near; he could feel the fluttering of huge wings around his heart, and yet his brain refused to accept it and his hand moved again towards the sound. 'Kill him!' someone shouted in the black-red mist of pain and he heard the boom of the shot like a faraway explosion. Something unbelievable happened in his stomach and chest and then he saw himself in a mental mirror as clearly as if shaving, his face a pure skull of agony. The image receded and he went down and down to the end of the black darkness. He groaned once and then was still.

'Tough bastard,' Johnny Boot said, dispassionately. 'Shore took a lot of killin'.'

'Hold on, Johnny,' Mill said. They stood looking at the prone form in the long-shadowed after-noon. Angel's mouth opened; he groaned.

Mill's tongue ran nervously along his lips. He smoothed his pants legs with wet hands, then took a long pull from a bottle he was holding. 'I owe you somethin', friend,' he whispered.

'Let it be, Willy,' Boot said. 'Come on, he's finished.'

'No,' Mill said. 'Not quite.' And with savage and quiet preci-sion he began to kick Angel's body, picking the tenderest and most vulnerable points, aiming carefully, poising his thick body and striking with all his power. The first couple of times Angel grunted from the depths of his unconsciousness. Once he opened his mouth as if to groan, but a trickle of blood was all that emerged. After that, there was only the ugly thudding sound of Mill's kicks. Boot stood to one side, a sickly expres-sion on his face. It was a long time before the fat man stopped.

CHAPTER SEVEN

There are deep recesses in the human mind into which the spirit can retreat. Sometimes, if it retreats too far, the return journey is impossible, and the shell which the spirit still inhabits is taken somewhere and what it contains is pronounced insane. Sometimes, in terrible illness, the pain will cause a similar retreat, for the darkness is safe and coming back means facing the agony that awaits. In such cases, a man will often will himself over the black borderline into death; or the physicians attending him will write on the charts they keep to show that it is not their fault: *do not resuscitate.* The endless capabilities of the human body are not measurable. There is a blackness beyond the darkness of pain and close to death, and men have been there and returned. Angel was in such a place.

Somewhere in that darkness he felt something. He knew instinctively what it was and he knew that he must move back towards the light. In whatever part of his brain the decision was made, a battery of warnings was flashed by other parts of his consciousness which warned him to stay where he was in the safe blackness, quiet and undisturbed. The warnings spoke of the awaiting pain and yet the faint spark that was life insisted that he try. He knew that he must try and he came back in terrible fear for then he knew that he must face the pain.

Even as he came up from where he was he felt the pain start, but he kept on coming and the pain came more strongly as he did but now his brain had identified the sensation he had felt and he opened his eyes to see it, even as his broken nostrils registered the rank carrion smell of the buzzard sitting on the ground near his head, beady eyes alert, beak poised for the first stabbing peck at his eyes. He drew a deep and ragged breath and the waiting pains came together in a crescendo that made him scream in agony and spiral back down into the blackness. It was enough; his trailing scream startled the huge black bird, which soared upwards in a tight circle, cackling in

34

panic, swooping to join a screeching trio of its brothers on the whitened branches of a dead iron-wood tree.

He felt as if he had been in the blackness for a long time, but it was only a few minutes before he opened his eyes again. Once more, the pain came; but this time he was ready for it, knew it for the enemy it was. A sound emerged from his mouth that might have been a curse or a prayer. He was lying face down on the rock-strewn sand, and the sun was brightening the arroyo. It was not hot. He thought about it for a long time and then spoke. The word was without meaning, but what he said was 'morning.' Then hearing came, and he heard the myriad buzz of flies around the patch of sticky, half-dried blood beneath his body. He heard the steady screech of the buzzards in the ironwood tree.

Morning. He had lain there all night. That coyotes had not ripped his body open he could only attribute to the possibility that even during his deep unconsciousness he had stirred, or groaned. Any movement at all would have been enough to keep the cowardly predators away. But they would not have gone far. He pictured them sitting at a safe distance, tongues lolling, waiting. The buzzards screeched monotonously. 'Yes,' he said to himself.

Getting his body turned over and levering himself into a half-sitting position took him the best part of half an hour, a half hour of the most excruciating agony. Head reeling, no strength in his arms, he lay gasping on the ground as the sun climbed up into the molten sky and seared his skin. Slowly he let the signals come to his brain, noting them as dispassionately as a surgeon.

His right arm was numb, the wrist a puffy, swollen mass of purple and black bruises. Flexing his fingers carefully, he awaited the screeching pain of broken bone. None came. He nodded. Good. The effort had exhausted him. He lay down again. Time passed, time without meaning. He hitched his body around until he lay half curled on the ground and could see his own body. With the stronger fingers of his left hand he tore away the bloodsoaked shirt and forced himself to look at the wound in his middle. He was afraid and he knew it. To be gutshot meant days of blinding agony even if a man were near help. Out here . . . he shut his mind to that. It would have been easy then to lie back and let the whole world slide away, let death rise in him like water at a dam, slowly, lapping him in cold oblivion. All he had to do was let go. Then the memory of the voice that he had heard come back to him and he knew he remembered it. Johnny Boot! He thought carefully of the man's face, fixing it in his mind, sorting out the features the way a drunken man will go through a bunch of keys. He saw Boot's face clearly; visualized him pulling the trigger, saying 'Tough bastard.' Then he let the hatred seep slowly into him, growing, funneling along his veins, building to a force that made him move deliberately for the first time. And then he knew that he wanted to live. He would live to kill Boot. He nodded idiotically as if someone had spoken the words to him, and the feral smile of a wolf touched his broken mouth. Yes, he told himself. He would live. Then he started to work out what he had to do.

He lay quietly for another five or ten minutes, although he had no real conception of time. He closed his eyes and ears to everything else. Then he sat up again, moving very slowly and carefully, testing himself against the pains, moving only against the ones he knew he could control. He took a longer look at the wound in his middle, forcing himself to accept whatever he found. The bullet wound was low on the right side, just below the ribcage and about three inches in. It had torn through his body. He reached behind himself with the good left hand, fingers finding the mush of the ragged exit hole. He traced its outlines; about the size of a spur rowel, slick with blood but as far as he could tell not pumping blood steadily. A clean wound. He was weak from loss of blood, but the bullet had gone through him. He nodded, and looked around. Something moved in the clumped ocatillo, and he went cold with fear. But then he saw the grey black pelt and knew it was a coyote. The buzzards still watched. He shook his head. 'Not me, you don't,' the movement said. His horse was gone. They had stripped him of his gunbelt and empty gun, and taken his boots. *They? Two of them? What did he remember? Something. There must have been two of them. And that meant Mill was the other one. Boot and Mill. Tweedledum and Tweedledee, Blackstone had called them. Yes.*

He swung his legs around and nearly blacked out again from the surge of pain that racked his frame. Ribs, he thought. He moved both shoulders up and down, very easily. Nothing grated, although the pain was intense. Maybe nothing's busted. He sure as hell hoped not. The thought of a broken rib end spearing into his lung ... no, he would not think about that, either. His glance moved all around him. They had left nothing. He was barefoot, a long way from anywhere, weaponless, without water, busted up. He had not drunk anything for almost two days. He knew there was little hope of surviving another. Only his iron constitution had brought him through as far as this. Then he remembered where he was. The arroyo! He turned on his left side and began to scoop at the sand with his good hand. The pain raced through him like liquid fire, but he ignored it, scooping away with bleeding fingers at the gritty desert sand, widening the hole, the earth beneath gradually becoming firmer, then after a while a shade darker. He kept on with the intense determination of the totally insane.

After more than an hour of this, every drop of moisture in his body had been leeched out, and he felt the soft dribble of blood from the wound in his side. But in that moment, he felt the trickle of water on his fingers, and into the hole he had dug a brown liquid seeped, about an inch deep, settling, even as he looked, back into the sand. He scrabbled at the wet sand, pawing it up and away from him and the water seeped slowly back. Ripping off his shirt he pushed it into the hole and clamped the wet rags to his broken lips. The relief it brought was almost sexual. He swabbed at his side with the wet shirt, wiping away the blood, cleaning the entrance wound and the larger exit hole. Then he padded the shirt and wedged it in his belt so that the damp part was against the wound at the back. His whole body and mind alert and refreshed by the few drops of liquid, he resumed his digging. In another half hour, he had a respectable-sized pool of brackish water. He drank sparingly. Too much water now could kill him. He washed himself all over, soaking as much of his clothing as he could with water, trying in the most elementary way to replace the body fluids he had yielded to the merciless sun. By late afternoon he was sitting up without trouble, eased of the terrifying dryness which had made his tongue cleave to the roof of his mouth, swollen and immovable.

'Now,' he said to himself. 'You're a big, tough man, Angel. Whip your weight in wildcats. Strong men grow pale when you walk into the room. OK, let's see you stand up.'

When he was on his feet the world reeled for a few moments and then his vision cleared. He had felt something like a slick internal ball bearing moving, and knew his wound had opened up again, and a moment later the soft trickle of blood tickled his skin. He shrugged fatalistically. The bleeding wasn't heavy: he could stand it. How much blood had he lost altogether? No way of knowing. What difference anyway? He might die if he started traveling. He was dead for sure if he didn't.

He tottered a few weak steps. God, he could hardly walk! The sharp stones cut his feet through the socks. The heat was terrible. The throbbing, continuous pain was as bad as it had ever been. He found he was on his knees with no recollection of having fallen. The buzzards sat in the ironwood tree and waited and watched. They had all the time in the world.

Angel had a few things going for him that Mill and Boot had not known. His years as the Justice Department's special investigator had taught him a thing or two about being left weaponless. After his first few assignments he had visited the Armorer in the echoing basement on the Tenth Street side of the Justice building and explained his needs. It had taken a while to get what he wanted made up, but the Armorer had been enthused with the whole idea and had come up with one or two refinements of his own. Inside Angel's belt he had made a channel, and into that channel threaded a yard of piano wire with two ordinary flat wooden pegs at each end. Angel unthreaded the wire now, dangling it from his good left arm. He then unclipped the belt buckle, which split into two halves; between them was a wafer-thin metal square with two razor sharp edges, made of Solingen steel. He found a fallen branch about three feet long beneath the ironwood tree which was more or less straight. Slitting it with the square of steel and then putting the square into the slit, one corner pointing outwards, he bound the wire around the neck of what was now his makeshift spear. If he had had his boots, he would also have had the pair of fine flat throwing knives which were stitched into the sides. He felt better with some kind of weapon, even one as primitive as the makeshift spear.

Using the spearhead he sliced strips from his leather vest and made rough pads for his feet, tying them tightly across the instep. He had no way to carry water. He scooped down to the wetness in his waterhole and drank as much as he could without feeling sick. It would have to do. He took a sighting on the sun and struck out towards the south, following the course of the Ruidoso.

Every step was painful. He disregarded the pain. If it came so strong that it became a warning which he could not disregard, then he would stop. Until then he would forget it, forget everything like a wounded wolf which will kill itself to get back to its lair. He knew something about the capability of the human body: he had learned that in training with the Department. It could go on a lot longer than the brain would admit. The brain would suggest, persuade, seduce the body into believing it had nothing more to give, but there was always more. Angel was traveling on that now.

He went well for a while. But the sun was still his enemy. It seared his skin, blistering his unprotected shoulders and back. It leeched the water he had drunk out of his system. The terrain conspired with the sun to tax him. His feet dragged in the sandy dirt. Across the empty wilderness Angel staggered on, repeating to himself in a maddened mumble the name that kept him going, left foot and then right, left and right, left right, Johnny Boot, Johnny Boot. The sun swung over and started to slide down towards the mountains and still he went on at his wounded snail's pace. The leather which had protected his feet was ribboned by the glass-edged sand, and his feet were torn and bleeding. He needed food, water. He would have to stop soon. Sundown, he told himself. Stop at sundown.

The shadow he cast grew steadily longer and he knew it was time to start hunting. He left the open desert and moved down into the dry arroyo of the Ruidoso, seeking a certain kind of rock formation. His swollen eyes soon found what he was seeking: a weather-scored, many-creviced pile of rock on the far bank, with a flat and sandy patch around it. He waited there, slumped and motionless, until the sun began to sink. Soon, as he had expected, a sidewinder edged out from one of the cracks and moved onto the sandy patch, setting out from the coolness of its lair to hunt for its supper. It was about four feet long and as thick as his wrist around the body. He let it get out into the open and then moved between the snake and its rocky home. The snake saw him and kept moving towards a clump of mesquite and thin sagebrush, heading for shelter as he came after it. He jabbed the makeshift spear at it and missed; the sidewinder ignored the weapon, moving steadily for the bushes. He lurched after it; if it reached the bush it would coil and he would not be able to get in close enough. He struck again and the razor-edged buckle sheared off the snake's head. When it had stopped slashing about and lay still he skinned the body, using the buckle. He knew how to make a fire Indian fashion. It took him ten or fifteen minutes, but he soon had the dried leaves smoldering and a puff brought the flame to life. He piled more dried sage and ocatillo on the flame: it burned strongly, making no smoke. The snake he speared on a sharpened stick and cooked it, eating as much as his water-starved mouth could manage. It was hard to salivate. The snake tasted a little bit like tough chicken. It was food. He had eaten it before. A man could always survive in the desert if he knew how. The Apaches lived there. They had lived there long before the Spaniards came with guns, horses, and the means to make fire. A man could learn if he was willing to. Angel blessed the old Chiricahua scout who had taught him these things. The food gave him strength. He went to the river bed and tried again for water. He dug for a long time without luck. Too many trees, he thought. He would try further downstream in the morning. The fatigue rose in him like a black curtain and he found a notch high up in the rocks where no snakes could climb, and slept there. The night came, and with it the desert chill. He shivered, teeth chattering like castanets, as the soft desert wind scoured his unprotected skin. The sickness of his body came on him in waves. His feet throbbed, the raw cuts shrieking for relief as much as his blistered back and shoulders.

Angel grinned to himself, the grin pasted on him like a skull mask. 'Wouldn't do this if it wasn't for the pension,' he told himself, repeating an old Civil Service joke. He slept fitfully, thinking of his comfortable rooms in Washington. He dreamed he was swimming in the Potomac, the water soft and balmy on one of those hot, muggy days you sometimes got back home in June. He woke before dawn, shivering still, moving around, flailing his arms about to get warm. By daybreak he was already on the move again.

The sun started its climb up the side of the sky, and he looked ahead to the mountains, which seemed no nearer now than they had been when he started. He knew he must find water soon, and yet he lurched on through the wilderness, something driving him forward. It was nearly noon when Kate Perry found him, and by that time he was almost out of his head with thirst.

CHAPTER EIGHT

Kate Perry was twenty-four. She was not beautiful by the standards of the East, which liked its women to have 'flawless' white skin and a languid manner. Kate was a healthy girl; her cheeks were smooth, and the sun's caress had tanned them to a golden brown. Nor did she have the hourglass figure so beloved of the advertisements. Hers was a supple, natural body; she neither pandered to fashion nor cared for artifice. Kate Perry was a western girl born and bred, and no amount of schooling in the East could ever knock it out of her. And thus it was that when she saw the stumbling, sun-crazed figure lurching through the broken landscape, Kate Perry did not faint or scream or run away. She touched her heels to the pony's sides and jogged towards Angel. He saw her come and stood watching her with a wary look, the look of a man at the end of his rope who cannot take the disappointment of discovering that his last hope is some bitter joke played by light and sun on the desert. But when she called out to him, Angel knew that Kate Perry was no mirage, and then he let go, his body slumping to the ground. She slid out of the saddle, her canteen in her hand. Cradling Angel's head, she let some of the water trickle between his lips, snatching the bottle away when he tried to grab weakly for it.

'No you don't,' she said quietly. 'You'll have to take it easy, my friend. Who are you?'

He told her his name, his voice cracked with fatigue and pain. Then she saw the stiffened blood at his waist and the dark bruises on his blistered body. Laying his head back gently on the sand, Kate Perry went across to her horse and pulled a Winchester carbine from the saddle holster. Levering the action she fired the gun into the air once, twice, three times, in quick succession, sounding the prairie SOS which she knew would soon bring riders from the Perry ranch to her side. It was a system they had practiced many times, for she had come across dead men in this country before. The enmity between the valley ranchers and those on the high chaparral was perhaps dormant, but her father had drilled into her the necessity of always being within gunshot sound of help. She sat on her heels, gently bathing Angel's lips and head, until the riders from the home ranch reached her.

'I guess I owe you my life,' Angel said, trying to sit up in the bed. The feel of cool cotton sheets on his skin was like balm.

His blistered body had been treated with a soft salve that had taken away the agony. His wound had been dressed and bandaged. His horse had been found and tended to. And they had told him where he was: on the Perry ranch, about thirty miles due west of Fort Daranga.

'You don't owe us nothin',' George Perry told him. He was not a young man, and the years he had spent in this hostile land had left their marks on his face, which was lined deeply and saddle brown beneath a crown of crisp white hair cut short as any West Pointer's.

'Any man runs afoul of them varmints is lucky to come out alive,' he added. 'Folks say them two have been behind quite a few killin's in these parts.'

'Not to their faces, they don't,' said Kate Perry. 'The cowards.'

'Now, honey, it ain't cowardice to face the fact that a man'd as soon gutshoot you as take a drink,' Perry said mildly. 'Meetin' that Mill on a dark night'd like to turn any man's stomach. Say, honey, did you tell Mr Angel he warn't the first man you'd found out on the desert?'

Kate Perry shuddered, and the old man grinned a little.

'Don't like to talk about it much, she don't,' he said. 'She run across a feller out there a few months back. Someone done a real job on him.'

'It was awful,' the girl said. 'Whoever did it must have been insane.'

'Freeman, his name was,' Perry said, undaunted. 'First we thought mebbe some young buck'd been full o' rotgut an' taken it out on this feller. But he turned out to be some kind o' Gov'ment man. Surveyor or somethin'. Deader'n a door-nail, anyway.'

Angel let nothing show on his face. Kate Perry bustled about, smoothing down the rumpled bed-clothes. Her patient was showing signs of restlessness, and she chided him with a wagging finger.

'No you don't, Mr Angel,' she said. 'You are going to stay put for another twenty-four hours at least.'

'Aw, ma'am, I feel fine,' Angel argued. 'Besides, this much bed is about as much as I can take, meaning no offense. You've been mighty kind, but I got to get up and about.'

'You never did say what brung you into these parts, boy,' Perry said. 'Not that I'm pryin',' he added, conscious of the fact that it was sometimes best not to ask too many questions of drifters who might have the law on their backtrail and prefer not to talk about it.

'No, I'm not on the run,' Angel grinned. 'But I figure I'd like to do a little rising from the dead in Daranga just to see what those two do when I walk in.'

'I wouldn't advise it, boy,' Perry said softly. 'They're mean-er'n pizen an' twice as fast. You take it easy a couple more days. Get the strength back into you. Besides, Walt Clare is comin' over here tonight. Sparkin' young Missy there,' he said, bringing a flush of color to Kate Perry's cheeks. ' 'Spect we'll have to feed that big ox again. He can eat more'n a starvin' wildcat. Love that does it, I reckon.' He stumped out of the room, grinning, and Angel found the scenery engrossing for long enough to give Kate a chance to compose her features.

After a moment he asked a question.

'Walt is our neighbor,' she explained. 'He runs a spread south of where I found you – the Lazy C. He and I are . . . sort of . . . engaged.' The blush was back, mantling her cheeks.

'He's a lucky man,' Angel said – and meant it. Kate Perry was a pretty girl.

'Oh, fiddlesticks,' she said. 'You're just sweet talkin' me so I'll let you get up out of that bed.'

'It did cross my mind,' Angel admitted.

'You can get up at suppertime,' she said with mock severity. 'Not a minute before.'

'Then stay awhile,' he said. 'You can tell me a few things.'

'I doubt that,' she said with a mischievous grin. 'You get some sleep. Tonight you and Walt and Daddy can talk your fool heads off. Do you like steak?'

'If there's nothing else,' Angel said and ducked as she threw a pillow at him. She went out of the bedroom and he lay back, hands clasped behind his head. The Perrys seemed like decent folk, the salt of the earth. Men like George Perry had tamed as much of this land as was tameable, scraping a living from the hostile earth, defending themselves against the ever recurring Apache outbreaks. They would have been embarrassed if he had called them pioneers to their faces; but that was what they were. When the history of this country was written, their names and the names of thousands like them would never appear. Yet they were making this history – they and people with the same firm belief that one day this would be a fine country for people to live in. But it was the wild bunch, men like Boot and Mill and the men who supported their killing ways, who would be remembered. History had a funny way of enshrining the badmen. Go to Missouri and they'd tell you what a fine man Charley Quantrill had really been. The ordinary men and women he had slaughtered at Lawrence would not get into the history books, but Quantrill was sure of his place.

He dozed lightly, his mind still working on the factional problems he had already encountered in the Rio Blanco country.

When Walt Clare came into the ranch-house, it was as if someone had let in a big friendly bear. He gave Kate Perry a hug, whirling her off her feet as if she weighed no more than a child. He pumped George Perry's hand, slapped the old man on the back, told them he'd left half of a deer he'd killed and skinned out on the porch. He weighed Angel up carefully when Perry introduced them; wary of strangers, Angel thought, and probably rightly so. He made no attempt to ingratiate himself, concluding correctly as it turned out later that any such attempt would have deepened Clare's suspicions.

They sat down to a fine meal cooked by Kate, and afterwards, while she hummed gaily to herself over the dishes, the three men lit cigars and sat on the porch. Angel knew Clare had been waiting for this moment, and grinned to himself in the darkness when the question came.

'Where you hail from, Frank?' Clare asked.

'I was born in Savannah, Georgia,' Angel told him. 'Been kicking around most of my life. Texas, New Mexico, Colorado, Kansas. Looking for that greener grass. Never have found it, but I keep on hunting.'

'You know cows?'

'Some,' Angel said. 'But I'm not looking for a job, if that's what you mean.'

'You don't talk much like a cowman,' Clare persisted.

'I'm not, though I've worked some spreads,' Angel said. 'I work for the Government.'

'Territorial?' Perry asked.

Angel nodded. It wasn't strictly true, but it would do. He wasn't ready to reveal his real purpose here yet.

'Mebbe you can tell me what the hell they're up to back there in Tucson, then,' Perry growled, ejecting a finely aimed wad of chewed tobacco in the general direction of town. 'They shore as hell got me beat.'

'How do you mean?'

'Lookit, son,' Perry said, leaning forward. 'We been losin' cattle on and off this past three or four years. Nothin' much – just ten head here, twenty there. Same for Walt, right?'

Clare nodded. 'They pick 'em off neat as flies,' he said. 'We let 'em. Take an army to chase a couple of men didn't want to get caught in this country.'

'Easier to let 'em steal, yeah,' Perry added bitterly. 'Exceptin' that them steers is financin' Al Birch an' Jacey Reynolds and that miracle herd o' theirs over t'other side o' the mountains.'

'Sayin' it's one thing, George,' Clare said. 'Provin' it is somethin' else.'

'Exactly what I'm sayin' to Frank here,' Perry burst out. 'We complained to the law in Tucson – tried to get the US marshal to send a man out here. N'ary a sign did we see he even got our letter.'

'We sent a petition to the State senator, askin' him to look into things up here. Same result,' Clare added.

'Damn, we even wrote to Washin'ton,' Perry said angrily.

46

'Not as you'd expect them fat-assed clerks to know the hind end of a steer from a Gila monster.'

'I heard some about Birch and Reynolds at the Fort,' Angel told them. 'They have the contract to supply the Army with beef, I hear.'

'That they do,' Perry nodded. 'An' the contract for the reservation Injuns. An' they got a monopoly on tradin' with the Army through that store o' theirs up at the Fort. Top of that, they got the *dinero* to hire a tough crew so we can't make 'em no trouble.'

'Some of our men have been threatened,' Clare said. 'Nothin' heavy, you *sabe*. Just a general kind of warnin' – might be healthier if you was to take a look at some other part o' the country. You know what I mean, Angel.'

'Any of them leave?'

'A few, dammit,' Perry said. 'Nothin' spectac'lar. But we're gettin' a mite shorthanded with roundup time comin' along.'

'Where do you sell your beef?' Angel asked.

'Got to drive it clear the hellangone across to Seven Rivers in New Mexico,' ground out Perry. 'Sell to old Uncle John Chisum up there, an' he's too mean to buy a pisspot. Allus claims times are hard, prices down. A man's lucky to break even after a year's work.'

'Supposin' Reynolds and Birch are trying to sort of ease you out,' Angel asked. 'Why would they? What's in it for them?'

'Dammit, boy, that's what we can't figger,' Perry exploded. 'Takes a man all his time to make a livin' off this land. Ain't no use for farmin'. They got all the land they need to run cattle – more'n enough, God knows, between 'em. You got to figger it's just plain cussedness. They want it all just because it's there.'

'Still doesn't seem like a good reason to go in for extortion and murder, cattle rustling, all that stuff,' Angel offered.

'Hah!' said the old man. 'Then you explain it to me, boy, because shore as God made little green apples, that's what they're doin'.'

Clare stood up, stretching. 'George, we've chawed this over

47

a hundred times before,' he said. 'Never gets us nowheres. We just got to dig in our heels an' not be shifted. One o' these days them two'll give up on us and let us be.'

'When I grow horns,' Perry told him sarcastically. 'G'wan, go talk to your gal an' leave the real talkin' to the grownups.'

Clare made an impolite gesture and went back into the house, and Angel turned to the old man. 'Seems like a decent man,' he said.

'Fine boy,' Perry agreed, 'I'm tickled he hit it off with my Katy. Ain't no life for a pretty girl, takin' care of an ol' grouch like me.'

'I didn't hear her complainin'.'

'No, nor you never would,' Perry smiled. 'But I'd like to see her settled. I ain't gonna last forever, son. One day this place an' Walt's will be one big ranch. He'll have the muscle to give Jacey Reynolds and his sidekick Birch a run for their money, God willin'.'

They fell into a companionable silence, the cigars wreathing them in the good tobacco smell. After a while, Walt Clare come out on to the porch with his arm around Kate Perry. Angel stood up, and the old rancher peered at the two young people with a mischievous grin.

'You two done with your kissin'?' he growled. 'Took you long enough.'

'Oh, Daddy,' Kate smiled. 'Walt is just leaving.'

'Shore you won't stay over, boy?' Perry asked. 'You're more than welcome.'

'I know it, George,' Clare said. 'But I got some stuff to do early tomorrow. I better get back. Mr Angel, glad to meet you. If you stay around these parts, come on over an' visit my place. Be glad to have you.'

'I might just do that,' Angel said. 'Thanks.'

Clare nodded, and went down the steps to the corral, with Kate tagging along.

'He likes you,' Perry observed. 'Don't often take to strangers. Mebbe thinks they'll give him some competition for Katy.' He chuckled to himself at the thought and went into the house. After a moment, Kate Perry came back into the pool of light, turning to where they could hear the sound of Clare's horse moving off across the packed earth of the yard. Kate waved at the darkness and they heard Clare call something which the wind snatched away.

'He's got a long way to ride,' Angel said.

'He likes to ride at night,' Kate told him. 'Says he feels closer to the stars.' Then she shook her head impatiently. 'That sounds silly, I guess.'

Angel shook his head. 'I don't think so. Neither do you, I'd imagine.'

Her smile was radiant. 'I'm glad you liked him. He said you seemed like a decent man. Worth saving, his words were.'

He was about to reply when they heard the boom of a rifle somewhere in the darkness. The flatter reply of a sixgun sounded. Then the rifle boomed again with a terrible finality that was followed by an immense silence. The cicadas had stopped their ceaseless racket and Kate Perry's face was chalk white in the lamplight spilling from the open door. George Perry stumbled out of the house, his hair tousled.

'What in the name of Christ was that?' he barked.

Then he saw his daughter's face and without another word he ran across the yard towards the corral. Shouting for his men to follow him, he was in the saddle and galloping off into the darkness before the tears that had been brimming behind Kate Perry's eyes finally spilled down her face.

CHAPTER NINE

Al Birch sat in his customary chair in the Alhambra Saloon in Daranga and chomped on his cigar. He was a big man, strongly built, his shock of hair iron grey, his eyes hidden beneath heavy brows and bushy eyebrows. Opposite Birch sat his neighbor and partner Jacey Reynolds. A thin-faced man, his nose long and drooping, Reynolds had the air of an unsuccessful undertaker. Both men had come to Arizona with the California Column during the War between the States, and stayed on. There wasn't an officer above the rank of lieutenant in the Territory of Arizona that one or both of them didn't know personally. They had used those friendships ruthlessly to carve themselves a monopoly in the Rio Blanco country. The saloon they were sitting in, their ranches, the trading post on the Fort, stores and hotel in town, all belonged to either Reynolds or Birch or both. They drank only good liquor, smoked only the best tobacco, rode fine horses. And they knew their power.

'This Angel feller,' Birch ground out.

'The boys have taken care of that by now,' Reynolds observed, pulling a gold watch from his fob pocket. His thin lips puffed at the briar pipe he rarely had far from his mouth.

'Thompson thought he might be another o' them Gov'ment snoopers,' Birch went on. 'Said he had that kind of look.'

'Thompson,' Reynolds said, and there was a world of meaning in the word.

'You think he was wrong, then?'

'I don't think I'd put any money on his judgment,' Reynolds said, 'but just supposin' he was right, so what?'

'Been a few of 'em,' Birch said. 'The Man got on to 'em because of his contacts back in Washin'ton. That Jasper MacIntyre that was sniffin' round the Land Office in Tucson. Freeman—'

'Hell, he was just some surveyor or somethin',' Reynolds said.

'Federal man, all the same,' Birch insisted. 'And what about Stevens in San Pat?'

'Boys found nothin' on him,' Reynolds pointed out.

'He was askin' lots of questions about sales of beef to the Reservation, just the same. You know what I say, Jace.'

'I know: once is accident, twice is coincidence, three times you better do something.'

'Damned right,' growled Birch, relighting the butt of his cigar.

'So?'

'Now this Angel,' Birch continued. 'I don't like it.'

'Explain,' Reynolds said patiently. 'What's wrong?'

'It ties our hands a mite. The Man sent word; we got to play it different, that's all.'

'Different? How? We can't pull out of this now,' Reynolds said, a trace of anger entering his tone.

'Agreed,' Birch nodded. 'But the old man says he wants us to be in the clear when we make our move.'

'That what he said?' Reynolds remarked. 'He's gettin' soft in his old age, ain't he?'

'Maybe,' Birch admitted. 'But this has gotta go as fine as snake hair, Jace. Johnny Boot and Willy Mill got to ease off. Or it'll get out of hand.'

'Mmmm,' Reynolds said. 'Might be wise. We need opposition now like a hole in the head. The whole thing could blow up in our faces if we play it wrong.'

'That's what I thought,' Birch said. 'Told the old man as much, an' he agreed. So he's sendin' his own man in.'

'Oh?'

'Said he was goin' to bring things to a head his own way, an' we was to make sure we had good alibis when his man went to work.'

'He tell you what he had in mind?'

Birch told him and Reynolds' eyebrows rose.

'God,' he said, sucking on the stem of the briar pipe, 'he's goin' for broke. Who's the gun?'

'Larkin,' Birch said, leaning back to enjoy the effect his pronouncement had.

The effect was electric: Reynolds sat up in his chair, leaning forward.

'Larkin!' he ejaculated. 'But he's—'

'I know, I know,' Birch waved his words down. 'A paid killer. Hired gun. Which is what we need right now. The old man is right. No more mysterious disappearances to bring in the law. No more o' that business of ever'body reckonin' it was Johnny or Willy but sittin' tight on account o' they couldn't do nothin' about provin' it. We'll be in the clear, all of us. Larkin will ride in and take care of things, and then be on his way. He's what the old man called his catalyst.'

'Catalyst is right,' breathed Reynolds. 'How come he's in such a hurry?'

'Somethin' to do with politics,' Birch explained. 'The old man reckons if we ain't got ever'thin' tied up neat by the end of summer, the word will be out an' we'll be left at the startin' post.'

'Perish the thought,' said Reynolds. Birch balked at his partner's ironic comment. Always some smartass remark, always that pretended intellectual superiority that he detested. One of these days . . . he choked back the bile in his throat and forced himself to smile.

'He'll be in on the stage,' he announced. Reynolds nodded.

'We'd better throw a dinner party or somethin'. Your place or mine?'

'Yours, I guess. Get Austin out there. Send somebody over to bring Sim Bott up from South Ranch – everybody knows he ain't mixed up in things up here. Make sure Johnny brings Mill with him. We don't want nobody wonderin' where any of us was.'

'Or the night after that?' queried Reynolds.

'As long as it takes,' Birch told him. 'Until Larkin has done what he's comin' here to do, we're gonna act like a Sunday school picnic.'

'That'll be the day,' Reynolds told him, and uncoiled his lanky frame from the bentwood chair, heading out of the Alhambra and into the sunlit street.

The lurching Concord careened into the plaza at about five, with the usual welter of noise and excitement, dust piling up as the ribbonshaker hauled the horses back on their haunches and yelled out his announcement. Only three passengers alighted into the street in front of the Alhambra. One was a whiskey drummer, clutching his precious sample bag and fanning his rotund face with a dustcoated derby. The second was a woman who was met by a trio of angular ladies who led her across the street to the boarding house, their voices trailing behind them like starlings on the wing. Those townspeople who looked upon the arrival of the stage as the highlight of their day watched all these activities with keen interest. The third passenger to alight was a man of medium height, thickset and mild in appearance, dressed in a dark business suit. Only his wide brimmed Stetson and range boots indicated his association with this country. His hair was a dark reddish color and his eyes were the palest of pale blues, almost colorless. He wore a white shirt and carried a small carpetbag. Those watching had noticed he tipped his hat to the ladies, and as he crossed the street towards the boarding house they summed him up.

'Cattleman in town to buy stock?'

'Don't hardly figger. Them ain't cowman's hands.'

One of the watchers, sharper-eyed than his fellows, had noted the thin, pale hands with their neatly trimmed fingernails. They were not the hands of a man who spends his life among cattle or for that matter the hands of a man used to hard physical labor.

'A drummer, mebbe?' opined another.

'No sample bag,' was the simple means of destroying that theory.

'Some business deal with Reynolds and Birch?' guessed another.

'Could be, could be.' The man had gone into the boarding house and their interest evaporated. Only one man at the plaza recognized the newcomer. Jacey Reynolds had been idly leaning against the south wall of the Alhambra, away from the knot of spectators watching the arrival of the stagecoach, his hat tipped forward low over his eyes. After a moment he hastened into the Alhambra.

'He's here,' he announced sibilantly.

'Good,' Birch said. 'Where'd he go?'

'Over to the hotel,' Reynolds said.

Birch nodded. 'Just fine,' he said. 'Set that dinner up.'

CHAPTER TEN

Nobody saw Larkin leave town. He had been told before he left Tucson that a horse would be left saddled behind the livery stable, and he swung into the saddle and moved the animal slowly away from Daranga, heading into the foothills of the mountains north of town. He had changed his clothes, and was now dressed in a dark brown shirt and pants, his scuffed boots showing no reflection of the early morning sun. The butt of the six-gun nestled in a cutaway holster at his side was matt black, and the Henry rifle in the saddle scabbard had been treated so that the nickel plating had no shine either. When Larkin moved against the landscape, the unpretentious brown of his clothes blended with the dun-dusty configurations of the land.

He headed up across the Twin Peaks and down the northern side of the hills, his destination firmly fixed in his mind. He had no feelings about the job ahead of him. The man who hired him had been succinct and specific. He had described the man Larkin was to kill with care and detail, and explained the man's work habits and patterns thoroughly. Together he and his employer had gone over the details of the trails, the topography, the pitfalls. He had never been in the Rio Blanco country but he knew it like a book. Larkin was a professional: he never got into anything without careful preparation. This one looked easy. Most of them did. Most of them were. It was when a man started thinking he didn't have to take pains that the trouble started. Larkin wasn't looking for any trouble. A nice clean job, the Man had said. One thousand now, another thousand when you come back and tell me it's done. Larkin grinned. A man could have a hell of a time in Nogales with a couple of thousand American dollars.

He found a stand of timber which overlooked the trail he wanted, and he staked the horse some way back where it could not be seen from either below or above. He watched the house below. It was a fine, well-built ranch. It had that solid, settled appearance of a place built to last by a man who intended to stay, and he knew from his briefing that George Perry was that kind of man, and could have built no other kind of house. He stretched out on the ground and watched the trail through a small pair of binoculars he had once won in a gambling joint from a 6th Cavalry officer. They were good field glasses. He could see everything he wanted to see. He watched Walt Clare ride in from the northeast, and from time to time during the evening, as the lights came on in the windows, he could hear laughter in the house below. He saw Clare and Perry and another man he did not know come out onto the porch. He waited, breathing easily like a cat waiting for prey. He saw Clare with the young woman whom he knew must be Kate Perry walk away from the house, and after a while he heard Clare making his goodbyes.

Larkin moved easily now, across the slope, quartering to the place he had picked out earlier in the day, his Henry rifle in his hand. He slid behind the fallen tree, easing the rifle up to his shoulder, and he waited in the darkness and heard the sound of Clare's horse on the slope below. Even in the darkness, the young man loomed huge. He was a big man. That much easier, thought Larkin. The looming bulk came into the sights and he followed it along the trail for a moment before he squeezed the trigger. He waited a moment, blinded by the gunflash, and cursed as a shot exploded down below. He saw the flame. Reflex action, his mind told him, I hit him right in the center and he went down. Larkin knew his shot had been a killing shot but he took absolutely no chances. He was already twenty feet away from the place where he had lain in ambush and he could see Clare on the trail, the skittish horse spooked by the gunfire but groundhitched by the trailing reins, too well trained to break and run. Clare was on his knees, and Larkin could hear the man's agonized coughing attempts to get breath into his shattered chest. There was not an ounce of pity in Larkin, no trace of feeling. He raised the rifle and took up the classic stance for firing. The bulky blob of Clare's body floated into the sights and Larkin breathed in deeply, then exhaled and squeezed the trigger. Again he moved, soft-footed as an Apache, twenty or thirty feet to the left, downhill. He was about ten feet from the fallen man. There was no sound, no movement. He catfooted across the intervening space and turned Clare over with the toe of his boot.

Larkin nodded. The man was stone dead. He ran lightly up the slope, moving into the timberline and back to where he had left his horse. He led the animal up to where the rimrock began and then mounted, letting the horse pick its way among the rocks, not urging it to speed until he had covered perhaps half a mile. He thought he heard the sound of horses back on the trail below, but by that time it did not matter: the man was not born who could trail him across those rocks. Larkin touched his spurs to the horse and moved off into the night. There was no satisfaction on his face, no smile. His eyes were empty as the night he rode through.

CHAPTER ELEVEN

Sheriff Nick Austin wasn't a good man or a bad one. He never thought of himself in those terms anyway. He was a man who held a political office which had been arranged by men more attuned to the nuances of necessity in politics than himself. He had a large family; he was not an athletic man, and he was long past the age when he could earn a living on a ranch for his beefy wife and their brood. When Al Birch had proposed that he run for sheriff, Nick Austin had been surprised and finally flattered into accepting. It was an easy job. Hardcases found Daranga a discouraging place; the presence of Johnny Boot and Willy Mill was enough to convince most of them that to move on was the better part of valor. So Nick Austin became sheriff and his office was, if not revered by the townspeople, at least tolerated. He didn't bother anybody overmuch and by and large that was how folks in Daranga liked their sheriffs. In turn, Austin repaid his benefactors by never asking awkward questions. He did what they told him to do and never did anything they told him not to do. In his years of office, Austin had grown steadily more corpulent and more lethargic; right now he was cursing steadily beneath his breath the fact that Birch had sent word to him that he had to attend Walt Clare's funeral. The lambent gaze of the high chaparral ranchers across the open grave burned into his tallow heart, and Austin shivered at what they might be thinking.

They buried Big Walt beneath the cottonwood he had planted himself to make shade on the ranch house. It was an overcast day, and a cold wind whipped away the muttered words George Perry was reading from an old leather-bound Bible as they lowered the rough pine coffin into the ground. When they were done they went into the house. One of Clare's riders took Kate Perry home; she had stood dry-eyed through the sad rite, her eyes dark with pain, welted shadows beneath them making her look haunted. No one had known what to say to her.

The men formed a rough half circle around Nick Austin and he looked from face to face, a sheen of sweat on his brow.

'Well, Nick,' George Perry grated. 'What you aimin' to do about this?'

'I . . . uh . . . I don't . . . ah, you said yourself there was no tracks, George,' the sheriff stuttered. 'What can I do? I could take a posse out an' scour around for days, an' mebbe then find nothin'.'

'Shit, man,' said John Oliver, Clare's foreman. 'You know well as we do who done this.'

'No, I don't know no such thing, John,' Austin said stoutly. 'I don't know no such thing.'

'Let me spell it out for you then,' Oliver growled. 'It was prob'ly Johnny Boot, or mebbe Willy Mill, or mebbe both o' them. Al Birch sent them up here night afore last and they laid for Walt an' shot him down like a dawg. Then they skedaddled back to Daranga. That's what happened, Sheriff. Now what you goin' to do about it?'

Austin drew himself up, his belly protruding above his belt, his face stiff with comical dignity.

'Now see here, John, I know you're lathered up about Walt's death, an' rightly so, but I happen to know that this time you got your reins crossed. It couldn't have been any o' Birch's men.'

George Perry pushed forward and faced the sheriff, arms akimbo.

'You fat impersonation,' he snapped. 'You askin' us to swaller that kind o' crap?' The sheriff retreated from the pure venom in Perry's gaze and the growls of anger which came from the assembled men. Angel got to his feet. He had been sitting to one side of the room, favoring his side, the dull throb of pain against the tightly wadded bandages a constant reminder that he was still some way from fully recovered.

'Hold it a moment, men,' he said, holding up a hand. He turned to face Austin.

'You sayin' you can show none of Birch's men could've done this?'

'I am,' said Austin flatly. 'An' who the hell might you be?'

'I might be Abraham Lincoln, but I ain't,' snapped Angel. 'Speak your piece.'

The sheriff drew himself up as if to bluster and then his eyes met the cold gray gaze of the stranger, and a chill touched the sheriff's spine. He had seen eyes like that before, and the man who had been their owner had been one of the coldest killers he had ever seen, a man in a jail in Yuma whom they'd told him had fought seven armed men with only a knife and come out of the fight on his feet with every one of the others dead. He had looked into the man's cell and the man had turned his head and looked at Austin and the sheriff had recoiled as if from the gaze of Satan himself. He did the same thing now.

'Uh . . . mm, ah, no offense, mister,' he managed. 'It's just . . . well, I happen to know there was a big party out at the Birch place the night Walt was shot. I was out there myself. Johnny Boot was there, and Mill. Birch, Jacey Reynolds, they were there. The colonel from the Fort an' some of his officers. Some bigwig political fellers from over Phoenix way. A whole swodge of people. There was a big dinner, went on all night. Hell, I'd've knowed if any o' them had been missin' long enough to ride up here, kill Walt, an' come back. It couldn't 'a' been done.'

'Nick, you better not be lyin' to us,' ground out Perry. 'You better be tellin' me the truth, you hear?'

'In God's name, George,' Austin cried, 'half the town was there. You c'n ask anybody. I'm tellin' you: they couldn't'a' done it!'

Perry looked stunned. He pushed through the rank of men around Austin and sat down, his expression revealing his total bewilderment.

'I don't figger it,' he said finally, shaking his head slowly from side to side.

'John?' He looked towards Clare's foreman as if he might be able to say something which would explain everything, but Oliver shrugged.

'I'm plumb bamboozled, George,' was his remark.

Perry got to his feet, stamping about the room angrily.

'But it's gotta be them,' he muttered. 'Who else would want him dead?'

Finally he stopped his pacing, and turned to face Austin again.

'Sheriff,' he said, 'I'm comin' to Daranga with you.'

Austin's eyes widened. 'There ain't no call for you to do that, George,' he expostulated. 'You can believe me. Why would I tell you somethin' you could check in ten minutes if it warn't true?'

Perry put a hand on the fat man's shoulder. 'No, man,' he said. 'I believe you. I got to go into town anyway. We need some supplies. Might as well go now, get it done. John, will you get a couple o' the boys saddled up an' ride in with me?' Oliver nodded and touched a couple of his men on the shoulder, leading them out of the room. Angel got to his feet.

'I'll come with you,' he said.

Perry shook his head. 'No need, boy,' he said. His voice was old and very tired. 'I ain't on the warpath. I might just ask a few questions around, but I ain't huntin' trouble. Besides, you better give that wound a rest. You ain't goin' to do it no good comin' with me. Anyways I'd be obliged if you'd . . . sort of look after Katy while I'm in town.'

Angel started to argue with the old man but he was adamant.

'I'll have Oliver with me,' he said, 'an' a couple o' the boys.'

Austin turned again to Angel, wary politeness in every nuance of his voice when he spoke. 'You been wounded?' he said, as if it were only of the slightest interest to him. 'Uhuh,' Angel said. 'Own fault. Nothin' serious.'

Austin nodded, reassured. 'I still never got your name,' he persisted.

'That's right,' Angel said, turning away. He caught the old man's eye and Perry nodded. Each man had his own way of skinning a cat. Besides, he liked the young stranger.

Oliver came back in. 'We're about ready, George,' he said.

Perry nodded. 'Tell Katy I'll be back afore sundown,' he told Angel. 'Try'n . . . well, you know.'

'Sure,' Angel said, 'I'll do what I can.'

'Thanks, son,' Perry said. He touched Angel's shoulder as he passed. Angel felt a twinge of pity when he saw the defeat in the old man's eyes. The sheriff glowered again at the uncommunicative stranger and followed the rancher out into the open yard where the riders were waiting with the horses. Angel stood on the porch and watched them as they rode off, until they finally disappeared behind one of the folds in the land to the south. Then he went down to the corral, where one of Clare's men had saddled the dun. The clouds were piling high above the Baranquillas. There was a feel of oppression in the air as the thunderclouds grew pregnant over the mountains. The chaparral was silent; no birds moved in the desert air. Angel rode slowly west towards the Perry ranch, trying to ignore the premonition that shadowed him, jeering.

*

George Perry rode down Fort Street and pulled his horse up to the hitching rail of the general store. Daranga was so familiar to him that he did not really look at it, and in truth, there was not that much to see. Fort Street was the upright of the T-junction on which the town had been built. Front Street was the trail that ran to Lordsburg in the east and Tucson in the west. On the right hand corner of the junction stood Birch's Alhambra Saloon, a gaudy place built as a direct copy of the Alhambra in Tombstone, which Oliver and his two riders had already gone into. Directly opposite it stood the boarding house, and next to that was the store into which Perry now stamped, slapping the trail dust off his clothes. Martin, who clerked in the store, and kept the books for Birch and Reynolds, came around the counter.

'Howdy, Keith,' the old man said. 'Like to get a few things.'

'Yessir, Mr Perry,' Martin replied. 'You want to let me have your list?'

'No need of a list, son,' Perry told him. 'I on'y need some fixin's. Bag o' flour. Couple o' cans of Arbuckles. Mebbe I'll take a few pounds o' bacon, oh, an' some o' that chawin' tobacco. I run right out.'

'Sure thing, Mr Perry,' Martin said. He wrote down something on a piece of paper, gnawing his pencil and frowning, muttering to himself. Then he looked up and said brightly, 'That'll be sixteen-eighty, Mr Perry.'

Perry nodded absently. 'Fine,' he said.

Martin looked at him and kept on looking, and after a moment the old man looked up. 'What in hell you starin' at, Keith?'

'Uh . . . well . . .' Martin managed.

'Spit 'er out, boy,' Perry smiled. 'I forget somethin'?'

'Well . . . uh . . . yes, Mr Perry. The . . . money, sir,' Martin said.

'Why damn, Keith, you know I ain't sold no beef this summer,' Perry said in mildly exasperated tones. 'Put it on my account like usual.'

'I . . . uh . . . I can't do that, Mr Perry, sir,' Martin stammered. 'Mr Birch, he done told me.'

'Told you? Told you what?' Storm signal fluttered in Perry's eyes.

'About credit, Mr Perry. It's nothin' against you personal, sir,' Martin's voice was greasy with embarrassment. 'I ain't to sell nothing to nobody on credit. Mr Birch said.'

'He say nobody, or me in partickler?' burst out Perry, anger coming strongly into his voice.

'Oh, no, sir, Mr Perry, he meant ever'body, I'm right sure he did. No credit, an' no exceptions, he said.'

'Damnation in the mornin'!' swore Perry. 'He knows I'm good for the money!'

'Yessir, I know it, Mr Perry,' Martin said. 'Honest, Mr Perry, it's nothin' to do with me. I got to do what Mr Birch tells me. You know that.'

'Now, son,' said Perry, controling himself and adopting a reasonable tone, 'you ain't goin' to make me ride all the way out to the ranch again for a measly sixteen dollars an' eighty cents, are you? I'll pay you next time I come to town.'

Martin wrung his hands, shaking his head simultaneously.

'You . . . you better talk to Mr Birch, Mr Perry,' he said. 'I got my orders.'

Perry's face darkened again. 'Damned if I don't do just that,' he snapped and turned on his heel, pushing his way past the other customers out into the street. He stood for a moment shaking his head in incomprehension at this latest evidence that the world was going mad, and crossed the dusty street on foot towards the Alhambra. He hardly saw the man sprawled in the bentwood chair on the porch, his feet out straight in front of him. As Perry walked towards the swinging doors of the saloon, the man, hat tipped forward on his face as if dozing, moved his feet as though by accident, and Perry stumbled across the man's legs. He put out a hand to save himself from falling and turned, with the puzzled anger from his encounter across the street brimming over.

'What the hell . . .' he began.

'You're a mite on the clumsy side, old timer,' said the man.

His colorless eyes beneath the shaded hatbrim bored into Perry's. The old man grinned, his good temper reasserting itself.

'Which I'm beggin' your pardon,' he said. 'Damned if I seen you.' He half turned to go when the man in the chair spoke again, his voice low pitched.

'You scuffed my boots,' the man said, mildly, 'An' I just had 'em shined.'

'Well, like I said, stranger, I'm plumb sorry,' Perry said, a trace of irritation coming back into his voice. What was wrong with the fool? 'Pure accident, no more.' He turned again to go and again the man's voice nailed him to the spot.

'Pure stupidity, you mean,' the man said. Perry wheeled, eyes glinting.

'Now look, mister,' he ground out, 'I done told you I'm sorry, which I am whether it was my fault or not, an' I'd say there was some doubt as to that, the way you're sprawled out like a daid frog.'

'You farmers is all the same,' the man said in that same mild, quiet voice. 'Born with two left feet.'

Perry shook his head like a taunted bull. This was incredible!

'Look,' he said, 'I don't know who you are or what your problem is, but I got no time to stand here jawin' about your boots.' He reached into his pocket and brought out a dime, which he tossed at the man. 'Go get 'em shined again, if you ever had 'em shined, which it shore don't look like.'

'You calling me a liar?' Perry looked at the man aghast. Suddenly all trace of indolence had fallen away and the man was on his feet, lambent eyes fixed on Perry, hand brushing the sixgun at his hips. Perry noted clearly in that moment how the butt of the gun was dulled to kill reflection, and then came the chilling realization of what was happening. Fear touched him momentarily but then common sense flooded back. This was foolishness, not a killing matter. He half lifted a hand, as though to reason with the man facing him.

'Now look here,' he said, 'there ain't no call for this.' He was surprised to hear his voice; it sounded dry and high pitched. 'No call at all.'

'You call me a liar and then say it's nothing?' The man smiled, lazily. 'Well, I'll listen to your apology.'

Perry drew in a deep breath and let it out slowly. He had no doubt the man was a killer: those eyes told him that. He must not be pushed into making the man move that right hand. The gun looked enormous. Perry's hands were wet with sweat.

'All right,' he managed, 'I'm sorry.'

'Fine,' the man said, 'now there's the matter of my boots.'

'Whaaat?' Perry's voice was strangled. He cast his eyes around. A few people had stopped on the street, watching the exchange curiously. They edged backwards. What was wrong with them? he thought. There wasn't going to be any gunplay. Oliver and his boys were only ten yards away in the saloon, for God's sake!

'The boots,' the man explained, patiently, as though to a child. 'The boots.'

'The boots,' Perry said, dully.

'Right. Good. You messed them up. Agreed?'

Perry nodded. He was speechless. There was nothing he could do. Where was that fat fool Austin? He had told him to meet him at the Alhambra. Where was the man? He thought of calling Oliver's name. But there was no way he could do it.

'Well, I'm a reasonable man,' the gunman went on, 'we can put it right in no time. All you got to do is lick 'em clean.'

George Perry looked at his tormentor as if the man had suddenly gone insane. His mouth opened and closed but nothing came out. He was lost and he knew it; the angel of death was sitting on this stranger's shoulder and waiting for the right moment to reach out and touch him. Perry swallowed the white ball of fear that clogged his throat. He was a brave man.

'You can go plumb to hell,' he said. He was astonished at his own calmness. The man smiled like a fiend incarnate.

'You better be ready to back that up, old man,' he said softly.

The moment stretched into an eternity. George Perry saw people in the street looking at him. Their faces were white blurs. His tormentor looked as relaxed as a cat in a patch of sunlight. I should shout for Oliver, Perry told himself.

'Like I thought,' said the man, 'full o' shit.'

Something turned in Perry's brain and he blinked as he felt the weight of his gun in his palm, drawn without conscious movement before the enormity of what he had done hit him. He stopped in mid-draw, the barrel of the sixgun just clear of the holster. The man facing him had not moved, but the face had changed. The smile had gone, and had been replaced by a mask twisted ferociously with the lust to kill. The empty eyes burned into Perry. He fell back a step. The gun was in his hand. He had not lifted the barrel.

'No,' he said.

'Oh, yes,' said the man.

Perry's hand twitched as though he would raise the gun and in that instant the man's hand blurred into movement, harder to see than a kingfisher's wings. Perry saw the muzzle of the man's sixgun and he saw the flame. The heavy slug caught him right between the eyes and blasted away the top of his skull, smashing the old man backwards into the rail of the porch, which caught the small of his back. He went over in a tumble of arms and legs, dead long before his body hit the dirt of Front Street. Something viscous streaked the wooden wall of the Alhambra. He never even knew that it had been Larkin who killed him.

The gunman turned to the people in the street.

'You seen that,' he rasped, flatly. The empty look of death was still in his eyes. One or two of them nodded, dumbly. They averted their gaze from the wall of the saloon and did not look at the crumpled body.

'Had his gun out afore I even moved,' Larkin instructed them.

One man nodded. 'That's . . . that's right, mister.'

'Tell it that way if anyone asks,' Larkin said and without another word he shouldered his way past them and crossed the street towards the boarding house, as Oliver came rushing out of the saloon.

CHAPTER TWELVE

Larkin sat like a lizard in the sun.

The bentwood chair was tilted back against the wall of the Alhambra, and his hat was pushed forward until it rested on the tip of his nose. His long legs were crossed in front of him and braced against one of the posts supporting the porch roof. A casual observer would have passed him by, thinking him just another sleepy-minded townsman passing a pleasant morning sunning himself on the porch of the saloon, maybe easing himself into the day after a hard night's drinking. But the people of Daranga walked a wide half circle around the place where Larkin lounged, for they had all heard now about the killing of George Perry, and they were wise enough in the ways of gunmen to know that the spot Larkin had picked was not accidentally chosen: it commanded a view up Fort Street and along Front Street, and they also knew well that Larkin was about as relaxed as a cat by a mousehole.

Larkin grinned to himself. Sheep, he thought. They had clustered around the old man's body like sheep, baa-ing to each other. He had watched through the window of the boarding house as the fat sheriff had panted up Fort Street and the tall thin man called Oliver had harangued him, waving his arms, pointing to the hotel. Austin had talked to some of the people standing around the body. They had nodded and shaken their heads and Larkin had sneered, knowing what they were saying. Sheep. Austin had come to see him, and their conversation had been brief. Self-defense, pure and simple. Everyone had seen it. There had been killing grief in the eyes of the tall man, Oliver, but he was not the man to take on Larkin, and the shame of his own fear had made the man almost weep with impotence. So they had finally taken the old man out of the town in a wagon, gone back to the ranch with his body. Now they would be talking up there. They always talked, Larkin thought. He knew their conversation as well as if he had written it out for them to read like a play. It was always the same.

But we can't let him get away with it, they would be saying.

Somethin's gotta be done, they'd insist.

The sheriff would tell them there wasn't anything he could do. Witnesses said it was self defense, he'd tell them. George drew his gun before the other feller even touched his. Half a dozen people saw it.

Well, damnation, someone would say, that ain't good enough.

And finally, one of them, his friend, or his foreman, or one of them who felt closer to the old man than the others, or one of them who wanted to make himself look big with the daughter would say, well, I ain't goin' to leave it like that.

And they would say, tentatively at first, you ain't going in after him, are you?

The man would say, half-defiantly, well, somebody's got to.

They would half-heartedly try to talk him out of it. People wanted something done, generally. They just weren't prepared to do it themselves. So there would also be an element of relief in it: that it wasn't going to be them who had to go and do something about the death of their friend. So when they tried to talk him out of it, they would only be half-trying.

Then the one who had spoken bravely would waver. He didn't really want to do it anyway. They had told him how fast the killer was with a gun. He would hope that his friends would talk him out of it.

Which they would now try to do. But not hard enough. So, having put himself on the line, he would not back down now. Nobody would say anything if he did, of course. But he would have compromised his own bravery and he would not be able to do that. He would feel he had to do it. He would even begin to believe he could do it after they told him how noble and brave he was.

And then they would say, maybe we ought to come with you.

He wouldn't let them, of course. He would tell them there were some things a man had to do alone. And they would nod, sagely, as if this were some eternal verity, and stand silent as he saddled up and headed for town.

Morons, thought Larkin. Sheep. You panic them with a flap of the arm, a shout. They see one of their number run and they all run. When the wolf attacks they cluster together and bleat. Together they could kill him, but they have no leaders. Which is why they are sheep. So now, these fools in the high chaparral; they will send in the best man they have and I'll kill him like a sheep and then they will have nothing left. And that will be that. There was no sense of anticipation in Larkin. He did not relish the killing. They were cogs in a piece of delicately balanced machinery. The Man had told him what to do, and briefly, why. He wanted those ranchers out of the high chaparral, and that was fine with Larkin. The Man paid well for what he wanted, and Larkin's job was to do it well. That way there would always be more jobs, and the money to spend time in places as far away from this ass-end of the world as possible. He thought of KayCee and St. Louis, and that time in New Orleans with the Creole girl. She had swung her hips at him in a place on Bourbon Street and he had danced with her until her movements had felt as if they were scalding his groin. He smiled slowly in the soft sunlight and remembered afterwards with her. That was the kind of thing a man needed. And this was a way of getting it. What was that thing he'd read? If God hadn't meant the wolves to eat the sheep he wouldn't have made the sheep. Something like that. It was damned good: exactly right. Larkin eased his back in the bentwood chair and let his breath out slowly. The sheep didn't even have to be chased: they would come, haltingly perhaps, but they would come to the slaughter. He knew that as well as he knew it was morning. He tipped his hat forward again and the smile touched his lips. All he had to do was wait.

CHAPTER THIRTEEN

Angel eased the dun to a halt on a slight rise north of Daranga. Below him he saw the unlovely huddle of the town, torpid in the blasting heat of the summer sun. It looked like any of a hundred other frontier towns Angel had seen: buildings of adobe or wood or both, with low adobe walls or slatted fences between the lots on which they stood. Two rows of buildings down the straight line of Fort Street, ending in a crossing line on the south side of town.

'Well, I see the dump,' Angel said to himself, 'but where's the town?'

He pushed the horse forward into a walk, moving down the trail that became Fort Street at the edge of the town, one or two private houses with picket fences, scrub gardens, then larger buildings: a restaurant, with the word 'Eats' on a swinging board over the door. A livery stable; a small adobe with a hipped roof and the sign 'Sheriff' painted on a wooden board above the doorway. The store, and beyond it the hotel, nothing more than a six-room shack, somewhat more sturdily built than other buildings on the street. The Alhambra on the corner with its ornate balcony and curlicued woodwork. They'd told him it was a copy of the gaudy palace built over at Tombstone, full of polished wooden bars and plate glass mirrors. Angel let the horse move easily, his eyes checking off faces on the street, letting himself be seen. Strangers in a town like Daranga were soon noted. He wanted to let the word percolate through. He reined the horse in outside a building which had a high flat false front and a shaded porch roof along the street side. There were no windows on the street, just a dark shaded door standing wide open. He went in: this was the saloon they had told him about, although no sign outside advertised the fact. They called it 'The Indian's' and he soon discovered why.

The bartender was short and swarthy, with a pointed black beard and opaque, expressionless eyes.

'What'll it be?' he asked. His voice was hostile.

'A beer would be fine.'

While the man pulled the beer, Angel looked around. The saloon was primitive enough. A long plank bar, a few tables and chairs, a faro layout at the far end of the room. Apart from one or two early morning drinkers the place was empty. The bartender pushed the beer across the bar.

'New in town?' he asked.

Angel nodded. 'Just got in.'

'Most people go to the Alhambra,' the bartender said. 'It's sort of required.'

'I'll get around to it,' Angel said.

The bartender's eyes dropped for a fraction of a second to the smooth-butted sixgun at Angel's hip, then up to meet Angel's eyes. He nodded, as if something had been said.

Angel lowered the level of the beer in the glass and sighed appreciatively.

'Good beer,' he said.

'Oughta be,' he was told, 'we pay enough for it.'

'How come?'

'Local monopoly,' was the reply. The bartender did not amplify it. Before Angel could speak again the door at the rear of the saloon opened and a small, dark haired girl came in. She was wearing a flimsy dress and her eyes were shadowed. She came up to the bar and her eyes flicked quickly up to meet Angel's. They were liquid, almost black in color.

'Let me have a jug of beer, Sunny,' she said, 'my friend's got a sore head.'

'Cash or tab?'

'What do you think?' she grinned. 'I'll take a beer myself.'

The man called Sunny served the beer for her and Angel turned as she raised her glass and said *Salud!*

'*Y pesetas y amor y el tiempo,*' he replied. The girl put on an automatic smile and moved a step closer to him, a calculated warmth coming into her voice.

'Well,' she said. 'You're a big one. Buy me a drink, stranger?'

'I thought you had a sick friend,' Angel remarked.

'Oh, that one,' she spat. 'He snores like a pig. He will sleep until noon if I do not waken him.' Her smile became ingratiating. 'We could go to the house of my girl-friend . . . if you like?'

'Maybe sometime,' Angel said, smiling to remove any sting

from his words. 'But I'll buy you a drink, if you will allow me the honor.'

The girl looked at the bartender. 'See? A gentleman, for a change.' She slipped an arm through Angel's, and tugged gently.

'What's your hurry?' she said softly. 'Stay and talk to Carmen.'

She was quite pretty. Small, black hair pulled back and tied with a ribbon, the body where his arm touched her breast warm and rounded. She smelled of soap and water, which in itself was unusual.

'It's a thought,' he admitted. 'But some other time, Carmen. I got to see a man.'

'Oh, let him wait,' she pouted.

'I can't do that,' Angel said. 'He's expectin' me.' There was a faint irony in his voice that made the girl raise her eyebrows quizzically but the words meant nothing to her and she shrugged.

'You are just playing hard to get, *si?*'

Angel shook his head. 'No, ma'am, I'm easy as pie. But not right now. Some other time, OK?'

'I'll be looking for you,' she said softly, and walked away, carrying the jug of beer on her shoulder and deliberately switching the hips only nominally covered by the thin dress.

'Quite a girl,' Angel remarked to the bartender.

'So they tell me,' was the monosyllabic reply.

'Friendly, too.'

'Like a bear trap,' said Sunny. 'Who's the man you're lookin' for?'

Angel looked up quickly. The bartender's gaze was direct and flat and his eyes showed no emotion.

'Feller called Larkin,' he said. 'You know him?'

'Know about him,' the bartender said. 'Killed a man here yesterday.'

Angel nodded. 'I know,' he said and the way he said it evidently confirmed something in the bartender's mind.

'He ain't no cream-puff, friend,' Sunny said.

'So I hear.'

The bartender shook his head, his jaw muscles working. He

71

stalked away down the bar, kicked a barrel, and cursed it fluently.

'Something up?' Angel asked, mildly.

'Ain't you got no sense, boy?' snapped the bartender, whirling around to face Angel. 'That gunslinger burns down old George, and next thing you come in to town with your guns oiled. Don't you people know he's hopin' that's just what you'll do?'

'Us people?'

'You're one o' Perry's men, I'm guessin',' the saloonkeeper said, 'though I ain't seen your face afore.'

'Name's Angel, Frank Angel.'

'That's fittin',' said Sunny. 'It'll look nice on your tombstone.'

'You must be Metter,' Angel said. 'They told me your bark was worse than your bite.'

'I'm Metter,' the man said, 'an' I ain't bit you yet.'

'Have a beer,' Angel offered.

'Don't goddam hedge,' Metter said furiously. 'You fixin' to mebbe invite Larkin to Perry's funeral?' There was deep sarcasm in his voice.

'We buried him last night,' Angel said quietly.

'Oh, damn, I'm sorry, Angel,' Metter said. 'I liked George Perry. He was one of the few decent men in this country. But gettin' more men killed ain't goin'to help.'

'Agreed,' Angel said.

Metter put his hands on his hips and glared at the man across the bar.

'Well, then?'

'I won't kill him,' Angel told him.

Astonishment flickered across the swarthy face and then Metter laughed, a barking sound of disbelief.

'Well, that's big of you,' he said. 'You've talked this over with Larkin, of course?'

'Come on, Sunny,' Angel said, 'what's eatin' you? You want George Perry's killer to walk away scot-free?'

'No, damn you,' Metter snapped. 'I just don't see no sense in more of you people gettin' your fool heads shot off is all. You're all like schoolkids with this eye-for-an-eye business. There ain't no percentage in it. Goddamn it, the man's a killer. He *likes* what he does, boy! You're askin' for it if you go lookin' for him.'

'You never answered my question,' Angel said mildly.

'What question, fachrissake?'

'You think he ought to walk away from this clean?'

'You need to ask me that? Then you really are stupid!' snapped Metter.

'Unfashionable viewpoint,' Angel went on. 'Way I see it, George Perry's death won't cause much mourning in Daranga.'

'Birch an' Reynolds, you mean? No, they're prob'ly plannin' to have a party to celebrate it,' Metter said. 'Don't mean everybody in town agrees with 'em.'

'But nobody's going to do anything about it, right?'

'Only a fool'd go against them odds, mister,' Metter said. His voice had gone surly and his eyes fell away from Angel's direct gaze. 'Nothin' much we can do.'

'Funny that this Larkin should turn up out of nowhere and do Birch and Reynolds such a big favor,' Angel remarked.

'What. . . ? Listen, talk like that could get you in real trouble, Angel,' the saloonkeeper said. 'Ain't nothin' to show this Larkin's got anythin' to do with them two . . . is there?'

Angel shook his head. 'Not as I know of,' he admitted. 'Strange, all the same.'

'I don't know,' Metter said. 'They wasn't no admirers of Perry but it don't figger they'd bring in somebody to kill him. Why would they need to? Why would anybody want him dead, come to that?'

'Or Walt Clare either, come to that,' mocked Angel.

'Listen, you're jumpin' to some mighty hairy conclusions, mister,' Metter said.

'Could be,' Angel said. 'Well, thanks for the beer. I'll have another one . . . later.'

'I'll pour it on your grave in Boot Hill,' Metter said sourly. 'It'll make the daisies grow.'

'My God, if you aren't mother's cheery little helper,' Angel grinned. 'Now I understand why they call you "Sunny".' His face grew serious. 'Listen. I need some help.'

Metter threw up his arms in the sign of mock surrender. 'Include me out, friend,' he said, exaggerated fear in his voice.

'Just tell the sheriff he's goin' to have a prisoner who won't be a bit pleased about the fact, will you?'

'Oh, that. Shore. I'll tell the sheriff that. He'll laugh, but I'll tell him.'

'Attaboy,' Angel said. 'Don't fret, Sunny: there'll be no killing today.' And he was out of the door before the words had sunk in, and walking down Fort Street when Metter spoke, addressing the ceiling or some other being in that general direction.

'How the hell is he so sure of that?'

Angel had stayed in Metter's saloon longer than necessary but he knew how it was in towns like Daranga: the word would have rapidly been passed that there was an armed stranger in town. Larkin would hardly need to be told that this might be someone looking for him; and Angel was perfectly well aware of how the gunslinger's thoughts would run. He knew that Larkin was in some way a key to the puzzle of the deaths of Clare and Perry: not their physical deaths, but the motive. Clare ambushed, and by a professional . . . Larkin? Perry whipsawed into a fight he had no way of winning: Larkin. While during these events Birch and Reynolds kept their men in full public view, completely alibied for the murders. If the murders benefited them, in what way did they? If the murders did not benefit them, why had they happened at all? Why would Larkin ride into Daranga unless he had been sent – or sent for? And why would they send for a gunman when they employed Boot and Mill? He shook his head; Larkin was the key and so the next step was to face Larkin.

Angel emptied his mind as he paced down the dusty street towards the Alhambra corner. It was a trick he had learned years ago, the ability to remove from his thoughts any distraction, any apprehension, any trace of imagination: a man distracted, afraid, or thinking about the possibility of losing a gunfight could not be effective. He would hesitate; and he would be dead. As he walked he noticed that the streets were cleared; a covert glance at the windows of the boarding house revealed faces blurred behind the thick glass, and he felt the pressure of a hundred pairs of eyes as he walked towards where Larkin sat on the porch of the saloon.

Larkin looked as if he was sleeping but Angel knew that beneath the tilted hat brim the gunman's eyes were watching his every step. He moved without haste, and there was no threat in his stance or his approach, yet those watching could see menace in his very casualness.

Larkin eased his feet to the floor and sat up slowly as Angel came nearer, then stood and stretched as lazily as a cat, turning to face Angel, leaning indolently against the post which a moment before had supported his feet. An infinitesimal nod was acknowledgment of Angel's approach. Angel kept walking towards Larkin, and the gunman eased his shoulder away from the post and stood balanced easily on wide-apart feet, his weight slightly forward of center, hand poised near the dulled butt of his gun.

Angel stepped up on to the boardwalk beneath the porch of the Alhambra on the Fort Street side, pacing steadily towards Larkin.

'Near enough,' said Larkin conversationally. He moved his fingers slightly, and Angel thought for a second that the man was going to pull the gun, but Larkin hesitated and Angel knew that he was puzzled by his inexorable approach, waiting to see what he would do. He kept on coming, and cast his whole life behind the conviction that Larkin's vanity would make the man wait for his, Angel's, first aggressive move. He was within ten feet of Larkin now and again the gunman spoke, his voice sibilant.

'Near enough, I said.'

Angel kept on coming.

Three more steps and he was within arm's length of the gunman and still Larkin waited and then Angel was facing him and the gunman cursed as he recognized Angel's tactic and his tensed muscles reacted to the command from the galvanized brain. His hand blurred towards the butt of his gun but he was too late. Like a striking snake, Angel's hand had moved and the barrel of his sixgun jarred into Larkin's belly, stopping the man's hand in mid-movement, making his gasp.

'*Don't*,' Angel said.

Larkin looked into the cold grey eyes and saw the killing machinery held in check behind them. For a long second the two men stood in a frozen tableau and then Larkin sighed and opened his fingers. His gun slid back into the holster.

'What is this?' he said. There was no tension in his face at all. He looked suddenly relaxed and at ease. Behind his eyes was an amused reaction at having been tricked, and the supreme confidence of the man who knows that his aggressor has a tiger by the tail. Whoever this cold-eyed interloper was he could not stand there all day with a gun jammed in Larkin's belly. As soon as the gun was put up, the advantage was canceled and Larkin knew without thinking about it that he could beat this man to the draw.

'Citizen's arrest, Larkin,' Angel said evenly. His voice was loud enough to be heard by the people watching. 'For murder.'

Larkin threw back his head and laughed, a good big hearty laugh of pure contempt and his laugh was at a high point when Angel slammed him to the floor with the barrel of the gun. Larkin was out like a light before his body jarred the wooden porch with the weight of its fall. Angel looked down at the fallen gunman.

'He who laughs last,' he said coldly.

CHAPTER FOURTEEN

Things were happening too damned fast for Nicky Austin. Up till recently, it had been nice and quiet around Daranga. Throwing the occasional drunk into the lockup was one thing. Bushwhackings and gunfights in the plaza were something else again. And now here was Sunny Metter taking the utmost delight in telling him that some stranger had thrown down on Larkin and was bringing him up the street to his jail. Panic flooded Austin's brain; he wanted to call for help, but there was nobody to call to. Both Birch and Reynolds were up at their ranches in the valley. As far as he knew none of their riders were in town. Nicky Austin was on his own and he didn't like it one little bit.

He liked it even less when his door was kicked open and he saw on the threshold the stranger he had met the other night at Perry's place, dragging in the unconscious form of the gunfighter Larkin.

'Now look here, mister . . .' he began.

'Brung you a prisoner, sheriff,' said Angel cheerfully. He turned to the grinning Metter. 'You owe me a beer,' he reminded the saloonkeeper.

'Come over an' drink all you want,' Metter said. 'I never thought I'd have the chance to make the offer.'

Austin's eyes shuttled from one to the other. His jowls trembled. In his mind he could already hear Birch's harsh voice asking him questions for which he could have no possible reply.

'Now see here . . .' he began again.

'This man is a murderer, Austin,' Angel told him coldly. 'I know it and he knows it and now you know it. I want him in custody until the United States marshal can get across here.'

'I can't . . . uh . . . you can't . . .' Austin's mind raced around like a squirrel on a treadmill. 'You can't arrest people in my town, mister,' he squeaked. 'I'm the law around here.'

'You're a poor substitute for the real thing, you tub o' lard,' Angel told him. 'George Perry had as much chance with this one as you'd have with a cornered wildcat, and if that doesn't make it murder I'd admire to hear your definition.'

'Perry went for his gun first,' blurted the Sheriff. 'A dozen people seen it.'

'Shore,' said Metter, sardonically.

'We'll just hand him over to the Federal marshal anyway,'

Angel went on inexorably. 'He's got some explaining to do. About Perry. And Walt Clare.'

'Clare?' bleated Austin. 'What'd he have to do with that?'

'I ain't sure,' Angel told him. 'But I'm planning to find out.'

'Now, wait a damned minute, here,' Austin said, getting up from behind his desk. 'This town can handle its own affairs.' How could he manage this? He needed to talk to Birch before this thing got out of hand. He needed help. By God, he needed a drink. He licked his lips.

'Murder ain't a Federal offense, Angel,' he said, craftily. 'You know that.'

'Hiring an assassin and bringing him into the Territory is,' Angel said flatly. 'I reckon when this little birdie starts singing that's what his song is going to be about. Maybe he'll tell us whose idea it was to bring him over here.'

Austin shook his head. He needed time. A thought came to him.

'This jail ain't no good, then,' he said. 'See for yourself. You couldn't lock up a ten-year-old boy here. He'd be out afore you could say scoot.'

Metter looked at Angel and nodded. 'Damn place has been fallin' down for years.'

'There, you see,' cried Austin triumphantly. 'You cain't put him in here.'

'Get some cuffs and leg-irons then,' Angel told him coldly. 'We'll hand him over to the military at Fort Daranga. I reckon they'll be able to keep him quiet long enough.'

'I ain't got the time to . . .'

'You'd better make time, Austin,' Angel said coldly. 'You and I are taking friend Larkin over to the Fort, and we're doing it now. So get your fat butt into gear and do what I tell you or this town's going to be shy one misfit sheriff.' The lambent fire in Angel's eyes made the sheriff quail. He hastened to do Angel's bidding, and by the time Larkin began to come around, groaning slightly as he opened his eyes, he was firmly manacled, and Metter had carefully searched him for hidden weapons, bringing a deadly little snubnosed

Derringer from the man's pants pocket and a sharp knife from its hiding place between his shoulder blades where it had hung on a rawhide thong.

'A real sweetheart, this one,' he remarked. 'But his fangs are drawn.'

Larkin spat on the floor. There was a trapped hatred in his eyes as he looked from Metter to Angel and back again.

'You're dead men,' he told them, a venomous satisfaction in his voice. 'No matter what happens, you're as good as dead.'

'Everybody dies,' Metter told him. 'I'd as soon be standin' up as bowin' down when it happens.'

Larkin ignored the words. He did not look at them again. It was as if they were not worth his attention.

'I'll get the hosses,' Metter said. Angel nodded his thanks, and jerked Larkin to his feet. The gunman snarled angrily at being manhandled.

'Keep your paws off of me, mister!' he snapped. 'I can walk.'

'Thank your lucky stars,' Angel told him levelly. 'I could have blown your gizzard out just as easy as buffaloed you.'

'You'll wish you had before much longer,' Larkin snapped.

'Talk, talk, talk,' Angel said, and pushed the gunman towards the door.

There was a small crowd out in the street, and they watched silently as Angel helped Larkin mount, tying him firmly to the pommel of the saddle. Austin bustled around, giving instructions which nobody heeded. He locked the door of his office with a great clattering of keys and considerable puffing and panting, then came down to the street and got aboard his horse. Angel watched the performance with grim amusement. Austin had told about twenty people where he was going, and why, and with whom. There was no doubt that someone even now was burning leather towards the Birch and Reynolds ranches: doubtless their espionage system was good. He wondered what effect the news of Larkin's arrest would have on them. It was for this reason that he had not prevented Austin from making so much fuss at their departure. If the two ranchers were behind Larkin's arrival in Daranga, then they would act. By their action he would know their complicity. If nothing intervened between their departure from Daranga and getting to the Fort, then. . . . As he turned his horse towards the northern end of town, Metter came jogging around the corner of a building. He was in range clothes, and wearing a gun. He looked like a totally different man.

'Hold up there, Angel,' he said. 'I'll ride along with you.'

'I'm thanking you,' Angel told him. 'You sure you want to?'

'No call for you to take sides in this, Sunny,' Austin said, pompously. 'It might cause you trouble later.'

'About time I declared my interests, anyway,' Metter said mildly. 'Whatever this is all about, I'm fightin' on the side that's against it. Which looks to me like you, Angel. I'm ridin' with you, and that's final.'

'Glad to have you,' Angel told him. Indeed, he was. In a tight spot, there would be no use looking for help from the cowardly Austin. The sheriff would either run or find a hole and hide in it until the trouble was over. Metter wearing a gun looked like a man you could depend on.

Larkin sneered. 'All of a sudden, ever'body's a hero,' he said sarcastically.

Metter looked at the man for a moment, and then spurred his horse until he was alongside the gunman.

'You know what, Larkin?' he said, softly. 'I hope someone tries to spring you. I hope they make a try. Because I'm tellin' you: the minute they look like breakin' you loose I'm goin' to put a slug right in your navel. An' Larkin . . . all my slugs got crosses cut in them. You know what I mean?'

Case-hardened as he was, Larkin's visage paled at Metter's words. Cutting a notch in the soft lead of a .45 made it a most terrible missile. Any man hit by such a slug would be torn to pieces inside as the tumbling bullet smashed through him. No one hit directly with such a slug could hope to live. And if the wound were in the belly . . . Larkin shuddered. Metter's mean gaze was direct and convincing. Larkin recalled that they called the man 'the Indian.' He didn't look like a man

80

who'd be too perturbed by doing just what he had promised. Larkin fell silent, turning away. Metter looked at Angel and grinned.

'Shore quiet, ain't it?' he said cheerfully, and pushed ahead of them, his horse leading the way up Fort Street and out of the silent town.

CHAPTER FIFTEEN

The sun was a red glow behind the far sierras and the dark fingers of night were streaking the sky before they reached the Fort. There was no perimeter guard; the Indians were currently quiescent, and so only a nominal sentry watch was kept. In its position on the fork of the trails, the Fort was by necessity a stopping place for travelers and traders moving between Tucson and Baranquilla, or on to Daranga and the New Mexico border. The party rode diagonally across the parade ground, pulling to a halt outside the Commanding Officer's quarters. The sentry outside snapped to attention and called out, 'Lieutenant Ellis, at the double!'

The young adjutant came tumbling out of the doorway of the orderly room – stopping mouth agape when his eyes fell upon Angel.

'You!' he said, disbelief in his voice. 'How the – what the hell are you doing here? You were—' He snapped his mouth shut like a purse and rounded on the young sentry.

'Over to the guardhouse and fetch Sergeant Battle and two men. On the double!'

The young soldier dashed away and Ellis wheeled to face the party.

'Now,' he said with grim satisfaction in his voice. 'Angel, who are these men?'

'The sheriff of Daranga, a prisoner and escort,' Angel said softly. 'Maybe we'd better see the colonel.'

'It's the inside of the guardhouse you'll be seeing, mister,' Ellis said.

'Thompson first,' Angel insisted gently. 'Fun later.'

'See here, so'jer boy,' Austin said pettishly. 'We been ridin' all day an' we're tuckered out. Ain't you got no respect for the law o' this County?'

'Not much,' Ellis said, 'if what I've heard about it is true. Who's your prisoner?'

'Feller called Larkin,' Metter said. 'Killed George Perry in Daranga.'

'Why are you bringing him here?' Ellis asked. 'He's not our problem.'

'If explaining it to you would do, we wouldn't be asking for the colonel,' Angel said. He swung down from the horse, and as he did so the clatter of footsteps announced the arrival of the guard detail. They came to a halt on the sharp command of the big sergeant with them, who regarded Angel with surprise and a sort of pleasure.

'Well, well, what have we here?' he wondered aloud.

'Sergeant, place this man under arrest!' snapped Ellis.

'What is all this?' shouted the bewildered Austin. 'I demand to see the colonel.'

'Aye, that you will, boy, just as soon as we've taken care of this one,' grinned the sergeant, flexing his hamlike hands.

'Sarge, I hate to do this to you when you're having so much fun,' Angel said. He stepped in front of Lieutenant Ellis.

'In the name of the President of the United States,' he said quietly.

Ellis took a step backwards. His was not the only open mouth: the others gaped at Angel, who had produced from a pocket inside his belt a leather wallet which held a gleaming badge. The flaring light of the lanterns on the porch picked out clearly the screaming eagle, the circular seal, the words *Department of Justice, United States of America*.

'What – what's this?' managed Ellis.

'It's called clout, soldier,' Angel said coldly. 'It means if you don't get out of my way you're going to be the sorriest lieutenant in the history of the US Army.'

'Department of Justice?' muttered Metter behind Angel. 'I'll be damned.'

'Didn't want to show you my hand till I had to,' Angel said without turning. 'This seemed like as good a time as any.'

He saw Larkin looking at him with a new expression and could almost read the thoughts which must be going through the gunman's mind. To be put under citizen's arrest was one thing. To be in the hands of the top government law enforcement agency was entirely another. Larkin was weighing chances and not liking the results. Angel smiled grimly.

'Bastard,' Larkin muttered. 'You bastard.'

'Not true, actually,' Angel grinned easily. 'But I know how you feel.' He turned again to face Ellis, who stood rooted on the spot as if paralyzed.

'Now, Lieutenant: do we do it easy . . . or the other way?'

Ellis nodded dumbly. He turned to go inside, then remembered himself. 'At ease, Sergeant,' he said. Then he almost ran into the colonel's office. Within moments Thompson's bulky frame loomed in the lamplit doorway. He peered at Angel as though he had seen a ghost.

'What's going on?' he snapped.

'I think we better talk inside,' Angel said. Thompson nodded wordlessly and led the way in. He took his seat behind the desk.

'You're with the Department of Justice?' he asked weakly. 'You . . . you should have told me that. It's unforgivable. I—'

'Colonel,' said Angel. 'We've had a hard day. All I want you to do is place this man' – he gestured at Larkin – 'under close arrest. I believe he is responsible for at least two murders in this area, possibly others. I know he gunned down George Perry in Daranga. If you want me to swear charges to that effect so that you have something in writing, we can do that.'

'Yes – ah – well, I'm sure there is no need for that, Mr Angel,' Thompson said, his voice still wavering. Angel caught the whiff of cheap whiskey on the man's breath. The revelation of Angel's identity had taken all the wind out of the soldier.

Thompson looked up at Ellis. His eyes held an almost pleading look. Ellis stared at the wall.

'Now see here, Colonel,' Austin said, wheedlingly, 'this yere ain't none o' my doin's. This feller just plain took over. I never knowed who he was nor nothin'.'

Thompson waved him silent. 'Perhaps you can give me some account of yourself, Mr Angel,' he said. 'How can I assist you?'

'All in good time,' Angel said. 'Right now, I want this' – he gestured at Larkin, who answered the movement with a sneer – 'in your guardhouse. I want a twenty-four hour guard put on him until I give you instructions to the contrary.'

'Instructions, sir?' snapped Thompson indignantly. 'On this post, I give the instructions.'

'We could telegraph Washington, if you prefer,' Angel suggested. Thompson let out his breath in a long sigh. He seemed to actually deflate before their eyes.

'No need of that,' he said, windily. 'As long as you can prove you're who you say you are.'

Angel produced an oilskin pouch and from it unfolded a document which he spread out on the soldier's desk.

'That tells you I am acting on direct instructions from the Attorney General of the United States,' he said. 'I can take any action to maintain law and order, civil or military, that I see fit. That means I can hold special sessions of court, empanel juries, subpoena witnesses, and even hold a General Court Martial. If I have to,' he finished quietly. 'It is your sworn duty to assist and protect me in so doing.'

Thompson sighed again, as though a forlorn hope had just flown. He had not missed Angel's reference to a Court Martial, as Angel had intended that he should not. Thompson nodded.

'What else do you want me to do?'

'I want your permission to talk to some of the men here,' Angel told him, 'in particular, Sergeant Battle. There are some questions I'd like to ask him.'

Ellis's head came up. 'What sort of questions?' he asked.

'Personal ones,' Angel replied uncommunicatively. 'Do I

have your permission?' He said it like a man who knows what the answer will be. The colonel hesitated only a second, and then nodded wearily.

'I can hardly prevent you,' he said.

Angel stood up, addressing himself to Metter.

'Can you see that our little friend is tucked away safe?' he asked.

Metter nodded, grinning. 'Bet your ass,' he said.

'What is this man's name?' Thompson asked, pointing at Larkin. Angel told him.

Thompson got to his feet and walked across the room to face the gunman.

'Where are you from, Larkin?' he said.

'Any place but here,' replied Larkin sullenly.

'You will answer my question,' snapped Thompson.

'Go to hell, you puffed-up bluebelly!' grated Larkin. 'I don't have to tell you one solitary damned thing!'

For a moment, the watchers thought that Thompson might strike the man. His face went purple with suppressed rage, and Lieutenant Ellis took a step forward, laying a hand on Thompson's arm. Thompson shook it off, spit forming at the corners of his mouth. He struggled with himself for a moment, then frowned as though remembering where he was.

'Take him away,' he said, disgust in his voice. 'Lock him up, Mr Ellis.'

'Sir,' Ellis acknowledged.

'Twenty-four hour guard. Day and night, watch him,' snarled Thompson. 'If he tries to escape, you will instruct the guard to shoot to kill!'

Larkin looked up quickly at the words, but said nothing. His eyes met Angel's.

'You wouldn't have set this up, would you?' he asked quietly.

'No chance,' Angel told him, shaking his head. 'I want you to sing, not croak.'

'Don't hang by your toes waitin',' Larkin said with a lopsided grin.

Ellis hustled the gunfighter out of the room, and they heard

85

him summoning the guard outside. The tramp of feet died away across the parade ground. Thompson went back to his chair, slumping in it like a man exhausted. He gazed emptily at the wall for a moment, and then pulled himself together.

'I'm sorry, gentlemen,' he said hastily. 'A long day. May I offer you a drink?'

Angel and Metter shook their heads, but Austin agreed noisily and Thompson poured two hefty measures of whiskey into two tin cups. He drank his greedily, then refilled the cup, setting it to the side of his desk. His eyes kept wandering towards it as he spoke.

'Perhaps you can explain all this to me, Mr Angel,' he said, struggling for some remnants of his dignity. His voice became pompous. He put on a ragged air of command which was almost pathetic.

'It's simple enough,' Angel began. 'The Department had several men looking into allegations of misuse of Government property and funds, on the Indian reservation and – elsewhere. There were also indications that a political group were creating a monopoly by coercion and price fixing. Nothing specific: but we were looking into it.'

'What happened?' Thompson asked. He looked very pale. He licked his lips and reached out for the cup, withdrawing his hand without picking it up.

'Somebody got wind of the investigation,' Angel continued. 'Three men we had out here were assassinated. One was knifed in an alley in Tucson. A second one was killed in what appeared to be a street brawl. A third was found dead in the desert; looked like some drunk 'Pache buck had killed him. Could have been pure coincidence, but we didn't think so. And whoever arranged the killings made a serious mistake, because they drew attention to what had previously been unsubstantiated reports.'

'Then how does Larkin fit in to all this – you sayin' he's the one killed those men?' Metter asked.

'Could be,' Angel agreed. 'He's a killer-for-hire, and those men were pros. They wouldn't have been taken by amateurs.'

'It sounds somewhat far-fetched, if you care for my opinion,' Thompson said pompously. He reached for the tin cup and this time gulped greedily. 'What on earth could be the basis for a conspiracy on that scale?'

'Money,' replied Angel succinctly. 'The high country ranchers have been systematically forced to subsistence level by having their cattle stolen, by having local markets closed to them, by paying monopoly prices for goods and services. Their men have been strong-armed – some have even been run off. Smaller ranchers have been closed out. And every time, Birch and Reynolds have bought up the land.'

'But why?' persisted Metter. 'Ever'body knowed Al Birch and Jacey Reynolds was land-hungry, but nobody could figger why. They had plenty o' land for the number o' cattle they was runnin'. They owned the store, the sutler's post, the hotel, the saloon. Why would they want the high country ranchland?'

Angel shook his head. 'I don't know for sure. I've got a hunch, but all I know for sure is that there's some mighty powerful politicking been going on up on Capitol Hill, and whoever is behind all the trouble out here has got people in high places under his thumb.'

'Do you – uh – do you know who any of these people are?' Thompson managed, his voice strangled.

'More or less,' Angel said, without emphasis. 'You only have to figure out what would be needed: then you can guess who they'd try to use. If we can get Larkin into court, my guess is we'll learn it all.'

'He don't strike me as the talkative type,' Metter argued.

'Let him think about spending the rest of his life in Yuma Penitentiary,' Angel said grimly. 'He might get real chatty.'

He stood up. 'I'd like to get started asking around, Colonel, before lights out – with your permission, of course.'

'Of course, sh – sir, of course.' Thompson lurched to his feet. They were surprised to see he was quite drunk. 'I'll get Lieutenant Ellis to accompany you.'

'No need,' Angel said. 'I can find my way around. Sunny, you want to check on our sleeping beauty?'

'Be a pleasure,' Metter said, grinning.

Austin looked from Thompson to Angel to Metter to Thompson.

'What about me?' he asked plaintively.

'Why don't you keep the colonel company, Sheriff?' Metter said. His eyes moved to the whiskey bottle on the desk. Austin's face brightened. He looked almost happy.

'That ain't a half-bad idea,' he said, licking his lips. 'I b'lieve I will. Colonel?'

'Do' min' 'f I do,' Thompson said. He nodded to Angel, dismissing him, and fell back into his chair. 'Make it a big one,' he told the sheriff.

When Angel and Metter came out into the open, they found Lieutenant Blackstone waiting for them.

'Frank!' he exclaimed, pumping Angel's hand. 'I wondered what had happened to you.'

'More than enough,' Angel told him, and briefly outlined the events of the past few days. Blackstone exclaimed in disgust when Angel described his ordeal in the desert.

'You think Battle knew about the set-up?' he whistled.

'Only one way to find out,' Angel said. 'I thought I'd ask him.'

'Angel,' Metter said, carefully. 'You ain't about to do nothin' silly, are you?'

'Who, me?' said Angel, smiling. 'Perish the thought. Run along, little man. Tuck your protegé into bed.'

'I'd as soon tuck him into a nice six by four hole,' snapped Metter. He faded off into the darkness, heading for the guard-house, and Angel started walking towards the stables. Blackstone paced along-side, a worried frown creasing his fore-head.

'Frank,' he said, hesitantly. 'If you're thinking what I think you're thinking, it's damned foolishness. I can't be a party to it.'

'All I want to do is ask a few questions,' Angel told him, with an air of injured innocence. 'No harm in that, is there?'

They were at the doorway of the stables. Inside they could

hear the sounds of the men caring for their animals; buckets clattered, hoofs stamped. There was an acrid smell of horse, urine, straw. Someone was singing *Lorena* in a soft Irish brogue. Angel went in. Blackstone hesitated for a moment and then followed. For a moment no one noticed them, and then they heard a shout of *Attennnnnn-shun!* and Sergeant Battle came hurrying forward, carrying a storm lantern which he held high to identify the visitors.

'Sir?' he said.

'Mr Angel wants to – ah – ask you some questions, Sergeant,' Blackstone said.

'Yes, sir,' Battle said. There was a finely honed edge of insolence on his voice which neither man missed. 'What would that be about, sir?'

'That day when you escorted me off the post, Sergeant,' Angel said.

'Ah, yes, sir,' Battle said. 'That day.'

'You made a very specific point of taking me west of the Fort,' Angel began. 'Why?'

'Orders, boy,' the sergeant said. 'Orders.'

'Whose orders, Sergeant?'

'Lieutenant Ellis was the one told me, as I recall. Not that it makes that much difference.'

'Plenty of difference, Sarge,' Angel told him. 'I was ambushed out there. Left to rot in the desert because some bastard had emptied my canteen and lifted all my ammunition.'

Battle frowned. 'You're not suggestin'—'

'I'm not suggesting anything,' Angel said flatly. 'I'm telling you what happened.'

'And you're thinkin' I knew about it.'

'Did you?'

'Damn your eyes, boy, if—'

'If what, Sarge? Go ahead, the lieutenant won't put you on report for speaking your mind.'

'I was goin' to say, beggin' the lieutenant's pardon, that if the circumstances was any different than they are, I'd beat your brains out for that.'

'You still didn't answer my question,' Angel said. 'Somebody wanted me dead, and tried to make sure of it. Somebody who had access to my guns and canteen. Somebody who knew there was an ambush waiting for me, knew you and your squad would deliver me to them, ready for chopping down. If it wasn't you, who was it, Battle?'

'Listen, boy,' the soldier said levelly. 'I told you once before I admired the way you stepped in when the lieutenant here was havin' a hard time with them two killers. I told you I had no grudge against you personally. Orders, boy. I was takin' orders. But I wouldn't take no order to set a man adrift in the desert without water nor ammunition, and I'll smash in the face of any man who says I would.'

'I never had any doubt of it,' Angel said, softly. 'But I had to ask. No hard feelings, Sarge.' He held out his hand. The soldier spat on the ground.

'Sure, there's hard feelin's, boy,' he said. 'Damned hard feelin's. You just told me somebody on this post set you up to be murdered. I don't want to believe that. But I'll take your word for it. And I'll be doin' my damnedest to find out who it was. When I do, I'll be comin' lookin' for you, boy. If you're shootin' your mouth off you'll have some crow to eat, or lose some teeth – I don't much mind which. Now get the hell out of my stables – I got work to do.' He looked at Blackstone defiantly – 'With the lieutenant's permission, of course.'

'Carry on, Sergeant,' Blackstone said. His face was red, and the broad smiles on the faces of the other enlisted men who had heard the exchange didn't make his retreat any easier. He followed Angel out on to the parade ground.

'You haven't exactly made Battle your dearest friend, Frank,' he remarked mildly.

'I know it,' Angel said, and Blackstone could see a faint grin on his companion's face. 'But if I read him right, the Sergeant won't sleep easy until he remembers who might have set me up. And when he remembers, all hell is going to break loose on this post.'

'You—' began Blackstone, but he had no chance to finish

whatever it had been he was going to say. A commotion across the parade ground claimed their attention and they saw men running towards a man on horseback who was yelling at the top of his voice. They ran across the square and when they got closer they saw a soldier running towards Thompson's quarters. The rider had slumped to the ground, and someone was giving him a drink from a water canteen.

'Fetch the doc!' yelled someone in the dark. 'On the double!'

Blackstone pushed through the knot of men surrounding the rider. The enlisted men fell back to make room for him and Angel.

'What's going on here?' snapped Blackstone.

'Dunno, sir,' said the soldier supporting the man on the ground. 'This feller rode right past the guard yellin' bloody murder, an' then keeled over. Look at his horse.'

The animal the man had ridden was lying a few yards away. Its sides were lathered with sweat, its flanks heaving; the horse was tossing its head wildly and neighing hoarsely, a grating sound of pain.

'Somebody shoot that horse!' shouted Blackstone. 'He's all but killed it anyway.' He knelt by the man's side as a shot rang out and the agonized wheezing of the dying animal stopped abruptly.

'Who are you, man?' he said, urgently.

'Hell . . .' the man mumbled. 'All hell . . .'

'One side there!' The men fell back to allow the post doctor through, and he took one look at the man on the ground and snapped, 'Hospital: fast as you can!' Willing hands lifted the man off the ground and hurried him over to the post hospital, where in the flaring light of a storm lantern, the doctor stripped the man's shirt away from his body. There were three bullet wounds in his chest; blood was flecking the man's lips. The doctor shook his head and straightened up. Angel pushed forward and went close to the man lying on the cot.

'You're safe,' he whispered urgently. 'You made it to the Fort.'

'Thank God!' The man coughed, bubbles of blood flecking his white chest. 'I – didn't think—'

'Save your breath,' Angel told him. 'Where are you from?'

'Circle C,' the man said. Agony twisted his features.

'Clare's ranch?' Angel said. 'What happened?'

'Hell,' the man said again. 'All hell. Broke loose . . . in high country. Raiders. They killed . . . killed. . . .'

'Raiders attacked the Circle C?' Angel said. 'Go on. Go on.'

'Cut us . . . pieces. And . . . Perry place. We . . . ran. Shot . . . all down . . . like dawgs. . . .'

The eyes rolled upwards and the man made a terrifying effort to come back from the edge of the precipice. His face was contorted.

'Get . . . help . . .' the rider said, his words fading away to a weak whisper.

'Get . . . help. All hell's broke loose . . . in the high country.'

And then he was dead.

CHAPTER SIXTEEN

Angel and Metter left the Fort long before the sun came up. Behind them they left the pandemonium of blaring bugles and shouted orders, the men being roused, horses saddled, preparing for the forced march across country to the ranches in the high chaparral. Traveling at their fastest, the cavalry would take two hours longer to reach the Circle C than two men riding alone, and that much more again to prepare for the patrol. To wait for them, Angel had stated categorically, would be to let the trail of the raiders grow cold and Thompson was not the calibre of man who could have persuaded Angel in such a mood to change his mind. Now the two men thundered through the pre-dawn twilight towards the Ruidoso, their faces grimly set against the thought of what they would find.

It was well after sunup when they reached the Circle C, but

they saw the smoke rising faintly long before them. The ranch and its outbuildings had been burned to the ground, the stock turned loose. Already the buzzards were at their grisly work. It was a sight out of the pits of hell. The black birds rose in a squawking cloud as they rode down into the open yard, where the bodies were scattered like broken dolls. They counted twelve dead; riddled with bullets, torn apart by close-range shotgun blasts. The awful sweet stench of blood hung in the air and clouds of fat black flies hummed in the sunlight.

It was not difficult to reconstruct what must have happened. The raiders had fallen upon the ranch without warning, and the Circle C men had died without a chance to fight. They had been cut down working in the corrals, in the outbuildings. The cook and his helper lay dead outside the charred ruin of the bunkhouse, obviously shot as they came running out of the blazing building. Nothing moved. There was a heartbreaking silence hovering over the place, and the crumpled bodies seemed unreal in the morning sunlight. Mass death is a strange thing: the unmoving bodies seem as though they have been posed, and will come to life if you watch long enough. Metter sat still in the saddle.

'Nothing we can do here,' Angel said. 'Let's get going.'

'God in Heaven,' Metter said. 'What kind of butchers done this?'

'There's only one kind,' Angel said. 'Come on. Let's see how much of an Indian you really are.'

'I can read sign,' Metter said.

There was no need of his tracking abilities. The trail of the departing raiders was easy to follow, for they had made no attempt to conceal it. It led, as Angel had known it would lead, up the rolling hill to the divide between the Ruidoso and the Feliz, almost due west, pointing straight towards the Perry ranch. They pushed on through the hills and when they crested the ridge, they could see the smoke down in the valley. As they got closer, they could see the house. It was still burning, flames licking dying tongues at what was left of the woodwork. The adobe walls were blackened with smoke. Metter ducked his head, cursing in a low monotone as they moved on down the slope and across the level land to the ranch. The Perry place had been caught as unprepared as the Circle C. The sheer savagery of the attack must have been terrible: they saw the body of one rider hanging face down over the low adobe wall around the yard before the ranch. The top of his head had been blown off at close range. Three men had forted themselves up behind a pile of timber at the back of the ranch building. Their bodies lay in a tangled heap, thick with blood. There were flies everywhere, and overhead the buzzards they had disturbed wheeled and swooped, waiting, waiting. Neither man spoke. They dismounted, and as if by prearrangement quartered around the charnel-place that was the remains of the Perry ranch. Both of them knew without speaking what they were looking for; they covered all the ground for fifty yards around what was left of the place before giving up their search.

'She's not here,' Angel said.

'Any chance of her being in Daranga?' Metter said, without real hope.

Angel shook his head. 'She'd have been here.'

'Then—'

'They took her.'

'Who?' Metter said. 'Who in the name of God would do this?'

'Plenty,' Angel said, 'if the money was good enough.'

As they stood there, a buzzard flopped down and waddled across the yard towards one of the sprawled bodies. Metter drew his sixgun, cursing, but Angel laid a restraining hand on his arm.

'Wouldn't do any good,' he said. 'And they might still be within earshot.'

'They're long gone,' Metter said, savagely, 'and it'll do *me* good.'

He fired at the bird, and feathers burst from its body, fluttering up and then slowly down as the buzzard screeched once and flopped over.

'We got some riding to do,' Angel said. 'Let's go.'

'What about buryin' these men?' Metter asked.

'The Army can do it,' Angel said. 'We got business with the living.'

He swung aboard the dun, and Metter put his hand on the pommel of the saddle, looking at his companion.

'You're a cold-blooded bastard, Angel,' he said, 'you know that?'

When he got no answer, he went on, 'Don't seein' this do nothin' to you?'

Angel turned. Metter gave a start of surprise, for there were tears in Angel's eyes. Or was it a trick of the light? He blinked and Angel was looking at the scattered bodies with an empty gaze.

'Sure,' Angel said. 'It does something to me. I was fourteen when Sherman marched through Georgia.' His voice was harsh and there was a savage glare building behind the grey eyes. 'They killed my father when he tried to stop them going into our house. Then they broke down the doors. I hid in a tree while they went in and raped my mother. She screamed when they got to her and she went on screaming for a long time and then she stopped. I sneaked in the back way and got a gun and killed a soldier who was standing at the top of the stairs fastening his pants. Then I killed the one that was on top of her. He didn't even know she was dead, didn't care. They came and got me and one of them worked me over with his fists. Then they made me watch while they killed everything that moved on the place: cows, horses, chickens, geese. Then they rubbed my face in the blood of the man I killed and rode off and left me there. Sure, Sunny. This sort of thing is meat and drink to me.'

Angel wheeled the dun around savagely and jabbed his spurs into the startled animal's ribs. The horse screamed and leaped into a gallop, rocketing up the rise away from the house. Metter leaped into the saddle and set off after Angel, spurring his horse to try and catch up.

'Frank!' he yelled, 'Frank!'

He caught up as they reached the top of the rise that sloped down to the northeast and away towards the malpais. The swath of hoofprints was wide and clear in the sandy soil. Angel tracked along them, hipshot in the saddle, no expression on his face.

'Looks like they're heading for New Mexico,' he said as they moved along. Metter nodded. He did not speak for a long time, but concentrated upon keeping his pace matched to Angel's, knowing they were punishing the horses needlessly, knowing the animals could not keep it up. But when the dun started to flag Angel whipped it with the reins, then later used the spurs cruelly, flogging the animal through the rockstrewn wasteland. Whatever was going through his mind, whatever dark thoughts pursued each other behind the burning eyes, he did not speak of them. It was noon before he pulled the dun to a halt beneath a stand of palo verde and dismounted. He slackened the girth, letting the reins trail. Water from the canteen gurgled into his hat: the dun drank greedily. Metter followed suit, and they turned the animals loose to forage. Range trained, they would not stray while ground-hitched.

Angel slumped beneath the palo verde, using the thin shade for respite from the blinding heat of the sun. 'We'll rest for an hour,' he said. 'No more.'

Metter nodded, trying to find a way to speak. Finally he gave up. There was no way to say he was sorry. He looked covertly at his companion. Angel's clothes were already filmed with desert gypsum, and his eyes were empty and fathomless. Metter thought he had never seen a man more surely ready to kill, and felt a cold finger of dread across his spine. Up to now, Frank Angel had seemed to be a competent, civilized, easygoing man who happened to have turned out to be a lawman. Now Metter saw him with the restraints of civilization torn off, the thin veneer gone, and the cruelly efficient killing machinery exposed. He wondered what Angel's life had been since that last year of the War between the States, what the man had done that had led him to undercover work for the Justice Department. Since by definition they had the pick of the very best the country had to offer, Frank Angel must be among a rare group of men. Yet there were laughter-wrinkles at the sides of the eyes, good humor in the normal set of the mouth. Angel didn't look like a killer. Maybe that was why he was what he was, Metter thought, but he let none of it show on his face.

After almost exactly an hour Angel got to his feet.

'Let's move,' he said, without ceremony. He went over to the dun, cinched up, and mounted. Metter followed suit, and they moved out across the featureless land.

By late afternoon they were in the malpais. The land no longer ran in long, sliding rises and falls, but was creviced and torn by meandering arroyos and strewn with boulders, scattered rocks, and sparse, stunted cactus. Ahead of them it shimmered with heat that made the land turn to water, distances disappearing into a haze that looked like a sea. Far off to the north, grey-blue on the horizon, they could see mountains. The trail they were following was hard to see now. They halted constantly, quartering across open spaces, picking up traces that men had passed this way: a broken stick of dry cholla stepped on by a horse, a pebble overturned and still slightly darker where the sun had not yet dried the cooler underside, a thread of cotton tagged to the spine of a yucca. The relentless sun reflected back by the mica sand of the desert baked them, drying sweat as it appeared on their bodies. They moved like tiny ants in some vast amphitheater of sand and wilderness, inching ever northwards, and always more west. By nightfall they were in the foothills of the Rincons, and everywhere stood the majestic saguaro, marching in irregular lines, looking like randomly erected candelabra, striking and red-tinged in the late sun, with the massive rock faces of the peaks soaring behind them. When night fell, they could go on no longer. Blackness came with the sharp unexpectedness of the desert, and they camped in a hollow at the base of one of the hills, shielded on three sides from the rear, facing south out across the tumbling jumble of country through which they had passed. They built a fire, propping a blanket on poles to prevent its glow rising against the blackness of the night, and huddled close to it against the chill of the night. Angel had coffee and a small pot, and they measured water sparingly into it, relishing the smell of it and the good warm full taste on their parched lips. Two strips of jerky made their meal. They fell into instant sleep, and it seemed to Metter he had hardly closed his eyes when Angel was shaking him.

'Up,' he said.

It was still dark; even the tinge of grey that heralds the dawn was not yet visible on the horizon. Metter shivered in the cold, as Angel fanned the small fire to glowing embers and reheated the last of the coffee. They had enough to take away the morning thirst, no more. They would need to strike water soon. Stretching stiffened arms and legs, Metter climbed reluctantly into the saddle. The horses, too, were still tired. They snorted in protest and bucked to show their disapproval.

Angel moved off down the slope, Metter behind him, shaking his head. He almost felt pity for the men they were trailing. He'd as soon have Angel on his backtrail as a pack of timber wolves, he told himself. They moved out of the hills and down the western slope of the Rincons, which they had quartered across. The faint trail had led towards the west. Tucson? Metter asked himself. About half an hour later they found the camp.

The ashes of the fire were cold. Two whiskey bottles lay glinting emptily in the sharp morning sunlight. Metter dismounted, stooping close to the ground, reading the sign he could see in the scuffled sand. Around the ashes of the fire the sand was churned and piled: some kind of disturbance: a fight? He said as much, and Angel hunkered down alongside him and nodded.

'Yes,' he said. 'Probably fighting over the Perry girl.'

Metter looked at him, sharply, but there was no expression of anger or regret on Angel's face: just that unemphatic determination.

'They were here night before last,' Angel said. Metter nodded.

'Has to be,' he agreed. 'They must have been travelin' hard.'

'This far,' Angel nodded. 'They'll ease off some now. They won't be expectin' to be caught up with.'

They moved out, down a long arroyo which led to a plain that stretched to the western horizon, speckled with yucca and prickly pear, the yellow scar of a wash visible about ten miles ahead. Far out ahead of them, blue-red outcrops of sandstone rose like the backs of whales. They strained their eyes but could see no sign of dust or movement.

'How far we come?' Metter asked, as they pushed ahead towards the distant hills. 'Fifty mile?'

'About that,' Angel said. 'We made good time this far.'

Metter pointed to the jumbled hills off to the south-west.

'Beyond there lies Tucson,' he said. 'You think they're headin' there?'

'Could be,' was the noncommittal reply.

'Reckon the troops'll have taken care o' things back in the Ruidoso country,' he offered.

'Uhuh,' Angel answered.

'You think they'll be able to follow this trace an' come on out here after us?' Metter asked. 'We run into them boys, we may need a little help.'

'Not likely,' grunted Angel.

'Chatter, chatter, chatter,' complained Metter. 'Trouble with you, Angel, is you talk too much.'

For the first time since they had come upon the carnage in the high chaparral, Angel smiled. It was a brief, on-off smile, but at least a smile.

'Thanks, Sunny,' he said. That was all. But Metter knew what he meant and felt warmed by it.

That afternoon they found signs of a second camp. It looked as if the raiders had stopped early in the day yesterday, perhaps deciding to travel in the cool of the night. They would be low on water, perhaps suffering from the extra thirst of hangovers, for there were more bottles scattered in the scrub. The sign around the campsite was much fresher, not dulled by the scouring, ever-present furnace-blast breeze across the desert floor. They were closer to the raiders now, and they moved more carefully. Towards sundown they came upon a long shelving slope of softened sand, where the shifting winds had drifted the streaming mica smooth across a stretch of flatbed rock, and saw the trail as plain as if it had been printed stamped into the gleaming whiteness of sand, curving away from the westward line it had been following, curving north and northeast and pointing across towards the northern quadrant of the Rincons and the tumbled peaks of New Mexico. They reined in and Metter dismounted. The lines of concentration between his black brows were deep.

'I don't get it,' he said, hunkered down gazing along the swath of tracks.

'Making it easy for anyone following,' Angel said. 'Or don't they give a damn?'

Metter shook his head. 'You have to try to leave tracks like that,' he said.

'Mile to one side or the other, you'd have trouble finding their trail.'

'This . . .' he gestured, 'this is like puttin' up a signpost.'

'What I thought,' Angel said. 'Take that side, I'll take the other.'

They ground hitched the horses and moved into the scrub on foot, keen eyes questing right and left, looking for any trace that horsemen or men on foot had passed. The ground was baked and hard, and strewn with rocks. There was no sign. They ranged further away from the horses, out of sight of each other, crossing and criss-crossing a central line drawn in their own minds, each line gradually diverging from the other.

Metter found it. They were now about a quarter of a mile away from the horses, invisible to each other in the gullied waste. Angel heard Metter shout. His eyes shuttled across the open land, pin-pointing the source of the sound. In a moment he picked out the shape that was the saloonkeeper, who was waving his shirt around his head. He was about five hundred yards away to Angel's right. Angel hurried towards his companion, oblivious of the detaining claws of the cactus. Metter's face was wet with sweat, glowing with triumph.

'Crafty bastards,' Metter said. 'Look here.'

He pointed at the ground, and Angel saw half a dozen pieces of roughcut rawhide, about six inches square, scattered in the lee of a sloping rock. Metter held a short length of piggin' string in his hand. He shook his head with reluctant admiration.

'They tied pads on the horses' feet,' he said. 'Led them half a mile, then turned loose.'

'How many?' Angel asked tersely.

'Two horses,' Metter said. 'One mule.'

'What do you think?'

'I reckon we're s'posed to follow the other trail,' Metter said, his teeth gleaming white as he grinned.

'You reckon they knew they're bein' trailed?'

Metter shook his head. 'Prob'ly takin' no chances. If the so'jer boys was comin' after them, they'd never find this sign. They'd hare off after the obvious tracks, bugles blowin' and spurs a-jinglin'.

Angel looked up, his eyes following the line of the tracks. 'What's up ahead?'

'Nothin',' Metter replied. 'More o' this.' He waved an arm at the desert. 'Then Tucson.'

'Right,' Angel said. 'Here's where we split up.' Metter just looked at him.

'I mean it,' Angel said. 'From here on in, I go alone.'

'Fat chance,' Metter said. 'Fat chance.'

They glared at each other for a moment, then Angel grinned.

'One of us has got to follow that other trail,' he pointed out.

'Hell, Frank, you know that's a blind,' Metter burst out. 'Razzle-dazzle, that's all.'

'Yes. And no,' Angel said. 'You dog that trail. My bet is it'll wind up in Grant Country, over the border. I'd bet that's where the scum that wiped out the Circle C and Perry's place were recruited. They'll be wanting to spend their blood money. I need names, faces, Sunny. I need them to make sure that no man who rode with that gang will ever do it again.'

'An' that means I'm elected,' Metter said.

'You see anyone else I can ask?' Angel replied.

'I'll do it,' Metter said. 'I ain't goin' to tell you I don't mind, but I'll do it.'

'Fine,' Angel said. 'Get word to a man called Mike Dempsey in Radlett, the County Seat. Tell him I sent you. Tell him the names, an' why he is being told. He can get help from the military at Camp Grant. I want those men in jail, Sunny.'

'I might just kill one or two of 'em first an' then tell this Dempsey feller,' Metter said. 'That OK?'

'Do what you have to do. Hand it over to Dempsey – don't try to handle it alone. Take this' – he handed Metter the circular badge of the Justice Department – 'you'll need to convince him who you are. Then head back for Daranga. My hunch is that when this pot comes to the boil, it'll be there.'

'When will you be back?'

'As soon as I've done what I have to do,' Angel said. He swung up into the saddle. '*Con Dios!*' he said.

Metter nodded. '*Con Dios,*' he replied.

He stood watching as Angel moved off to the west, steady and relentless on the faint trace they had discovered. After a moment he reined his horse around and headed back towards the sandy slope where the tracks of the raiders lay stark in the sunlight. When he looked back again, he could not see Angel. Metter moved on towards the mountains.

CHAPTER SEVENTEEN

Night had fallen an hour ago, and still Angel moved on through the desert. There was a full moon, and when the cloud broke, its silver light bathed the cactus, heightening their weirdness, casting shattered shadows on the broken

102

ground. Ahead the land broke, cresting into a high rise which fell on its western side sharply down into a shadowed arroyo. Angel approached it on foot, his hand clamped on the horse's muzzle. The hairs on the back of his neck rose. He knew, without knowing how he knew, that one of the men he was seeking was down there, perhaps both of them.

He took all the time he needed.

Belly down in the fine ground sand he wormed forward on his elbows and knees to the edge of the arroyo. Flints and broken cactus spiked his bare hands and tore his shirt but he moved on like a hunting snake, oblivious to the pain. He edged easily over the crest of the arroyo and slithered down. As he came down the slow slope, he caught a flicker of light along the canyon, hidden perhaps behind a bend or a pile of rock. With infinite care he moved forward again, until he raised his head and saw the dull red embers of a campfire glowing. A man was sitting cross-legged in front of the dying fire. Behind him lay a spread bedroll and a saddle ready to be used as a pillow. The man threw some twigs on the embers and in the quick flicker of a flame Angel saw that the man was Johnny Boot. The face looked strange, as if lopsided. After a moment, Angel recognized that Boot's face was bruised, as if he had been fighting. He inched further forward. If Boot was here, Mill could be nearby. He could now see the full flat base of the arroyo, and Boot's horse idly cropping at some thin grass growing precariously from the side of the wash. Boot was alone. He stood up and stretched, the deepset eyes like black holes in the high cheekboned face, the thin frame taut and wary even in repose. Boot unbuckled his gunbelt and laid it by the saddle, and then lay down without removing any of his other clothes. He turned to the right, and then the left, wallowing until he was covered by his blanket. Angel lay still and waited. He watched the moon sail by overhead and counted stars for a while. The Great Bear and the Little Bear, the Pole Star. Those were the ones he knew. It would be nice to study the stars, he thought. Inside his head a clock was ticking, counting the seconds as they coagulated into minutes and the minutes as they crawled by. After what he deemed an hour, Angel figured Boot would be as asleep as he was ever likely to be. Johnny Boot had been too long on the wolf trail to ever really sleep deeply. He would wake up instantly if Angel made a sound. With careful, measured movement, Angel drew his feet up and under himself. Very slowly, he got to his feet and stood fully upright. He drew in a slow deep breath and let it out as he moved forward. He was about ten yards away from Boot when the desert wind shifted around behind him and Boot's horse lifted its head and snorted a warning.

Boot rolled out of his blankets almost before the animal had finished blowing the air through its nostrils, his right hand snatching the sixgun from the holster by his head, eyes searching the blackness for his assailant. He saw Angel diving for the cover of the rocks, and the gun in his hand boomed, the slug ricocheting off the sandstone and filling the air with flickering splinters of rock. Angel rolled backwards away from the first hiding place as Boot scuttled across the open bottom of the arroyo, moving to another position as the gunman found shelter behind a tilted rock lying on the sloping side of the riverbed.

'Who the hell are you?' shouted Boot.

Angel remained silent.

'Speak, damn you!' yelled Boot. 'Who's there?'

While the man was shouting, Angel moved again. On all fours he slid halfway up the far side of the arroyo away from where Boot lay hidden. He heard Boot shout again and fire another shot, the report booming in the darkness, the flash muted behind the rock. In the moments of that noise, Angel was over the rim of the arroyo and on the flat scrubland above it, easing along on his hands and belly, his gun held ready but uncocked.

He heard a scuttling down below and peered over the edge. Boot had changed his position, and was now belly down on the sandy arroyo bed, trying to get back to his bedroll. Angel grinned: Boot had forgotten to grab his cartridge belt and had suddenly realized he had only three shots left in the gun. Angel's fingers closed around a big pebble and he tossed it up the arroyo behind Boot's back. Boot rolled over and faced the direction of the sound, ready to fire. In that moment Angel loosed off a shot which ripped the back of Boot's calf, tearing through the leather of his boot and searing the soft muscle. Boot screamed in agony and rolled away behind the rock he had used previously.

'Johnny,' Angel called. Up this high, he knew his voice would sound disembodied; Boot would find it difficult to pinpoint Angel's position.

'Who the hell are you?' shouted Boot. 'Show yourself!'

Angel could hear the man's muttered curses, could almost see in his mind's eye Boot's frantic efforts to staunch the flow of blood from his ripped leg.

'Johnny!' Angel's voice was peremptory now. 'Where's the girl, Johnny?'

'Angel?' There was disbelief in Boot's voice. 'Angel? Is that you?'

'It's me. Where's the girl?'

He heard Boot chuckle maliciously.

'What's it worth to you, Angel?'

'You're in no spot to bargain, Johnny,' Angel said. To emphasize his point he drove three bullets into various angles of the slanted rock sheltering Boot. The whining, disintegrating slugs and the splintered stone drove Boot down flat for safety, cursing as he filled his unprepared mouth with sand.

Angel rolled to a new position and fired two more rounds rapidly, the slugs angling off the rock, cutting through the air like demented hornets as they caromed. He reloaded quickly, letting Boot hear the sound of the chamber as he turned it.

'I got all night and plenty of bullets, Johnny,' he called. 'Where's the girl?'

'Go to hell,' yelled Boot, then ducked flat again as Angel blasted two more bullets against the rock.

'One of those slugs is going to find you sooner or later, Johnny!' yelled Angel. 'Better talk!'

Boot fired at the place where he had seen the gunflashes, but Angel was well away from there, rolling soundlessly to a new position. Each time, he opened the angle slightly more. It would only be a matter of time before he could bounce a slug off the rock and hit the crouching man.

'She's long gone, Angel!' Boot yelled. His laugh was maniacal. 'Willy took a shine to her.'

'Where's he headed, Johnny?'

'Go to hell!' yelled Boot.

'See you there!' Angel replied coldly, letting another pair of slugs smash chunks out of Boot's shelter.

'I can stay here all night, Angel!' yelled Boot. 'Why don't you show yourself like a man?'

Angel blasted the rock again and then again, rolling aside and this time coming near the edge of the arroyo. He reloaded. The gunbarrel was hot. He heard Boot shout as he moved, knew he had hit the man, but not how badly.

'Damn . . . you!' Boot shouted. His voice was thinner. Angel nodded grimly.

'Last chance, Johnny!' he called. 'The next one's got your name on it.'

'Won't do you . . . no good, Angel,' Boot said. His voice slurred a little. 'She's well broke. The boys . . . had their fun with her.' His laughter was touched with a final madness. 'All of us . . . bitch.'

Angel showed the man a target. He raised his head and shoulders up above the rim of the arroyo and then ducked down again in one smooth movement and Boot's sixgun boomed, the slug splashing the sandy earth a few feet away from Angel.

'One left, Johnny,' he called. 'How you liking it down there?'

Boot let fly with a stream of curses, calling his assailant every filthy thing he could lay tongue to.

'Sure, sure,' Angel called. 'You and Willy fall out, Johnny?'

'Damn you . . .' Boot's cough interrupted whatever he had been going to say. It sounded like the sick cough of a wounded man, but Angel was taking no chances. He moved now like a cat, stealthily through the darkness, swiftly across the open spaces between the looming cactus, heading up the lip of the arroyo fifty, sixty, seventy feet away from where he had been lying. Then he edged over the rim of the arroyo and slid carefully down to the base of the declivity. He crouched, sixgun ready, on the sandy floor of the dried river bed. Moving like a shadow, easing from one piece of sparse shelter to the next, Angel made his way up behind Boot. The thinnest streak of grey was touching the blackness of the sky. He could see the dark blob that was Boot slumped behind the rock.

'Let go of the gun, Johnny,' he said softly.

Boot did not move.

'Last warning, Johnny. Toss the gun out away from yourself.'

Still not a flicker of movement, not a sound. Was Boot playing possum? Angel drew a breath and moved out into the open, sixgun at full cock and trained on the slumped form of the gunman. Boot lay with his arm outstretched, the gun lying just beyond his splayed fingers. Angel stepped forward and kicked the gun away, and in that moment Boot came up off the floor, his other hand full of sand which he tossed into Angel's face. In the same desperate movement Boot rolled towards the sixgun Angel had kicked aside, his hand fastening on it, easing the hammer back. The barrel lifted towards Angel and Johnny Boot died with the evil delight on his face of a man who has pulled off something very smart, very difficult, sure that he had won. Angel's bullet smashed Johnny Boot flat dead on the sand. He looked down at the crumpled body, the anger still searing through his body.

'You died too easy,' he said.

CHAPTER EIGHTEEN

Their grisly duty done, the troopers returned to Fort Daranga. Thompson led them in, stepping down from the saddle and beating the dust from his uniform, then stamping up the steps into his office. Lieutenant Ellis came to attention behind the desk.

'Get me a drink, Mr Ellis,' the colonel said, slumping into

his chair. Ellis hastened to pour a generous measure of whisky and placed the tin cup on the desk before the grey-faced soldier.

'I've never seen anything like it,' Thompson said, as though to himself. 'Not in peacetime. Never.'

'It was bad, then?' Ellis prompted. He had stayed behind in command during the absence of the patrol.

'Bad, bad?' Thompson snarled, 'It was . . . it was . . . aaah!' He hurled the tin cup at the wall and pushed his chair back from the desk. 'I'm going to get a wash and shave,' he said. 'Get Sergeant Battle to give you a full report. I'll add my observations.'

'Before you go, sir . . .' Ellis said hesitantly.

'What is it, mister? I'm dog tired.'

'Jacey Reynolds is here, sir. He asked specially to see you.' The young soldier put definite emphasis on each word. Thompson looked up, his eyes wary.

'He say what he wanted, Peter?'

'No, sir, but I can guess.' Ellis jerked his head towards the window, through which they could clearly see the guardhouse across the parade ground.

'Tell him I'm in my quarters,' Thompson said.

'You want me to come as well?' Ellis put in, Thompson squeezed the bridge of his nose between finger and thumb. 'What? Oh, I don't know. Yes. No. perhaps you'd better not. Let me talk to him first.'

Ellis simply stood and looked at Thompson whose gaze fell, then came up again defiantly. 'Leave it to me. It's all right: leave it to me.'

'Yes, sir,' Ellis said. There was absolutely no emphasis on either word.

Thompson went out of the office and across to his quarters, returning the salutes of enlisted men he passed on his way. He went into the building, relishing the cool shaded interior after the furnace heat of the high country. There was a pitcher of water on the bureau, a damp cloth across the top to keep it cool. He poured a glass full, drank it, then another. Stripping off his field jacket, he let his suspenders down over his shoulders and pulled the woollen shirt over his head. His body was streaked with muddy marks where sweat and dirt had mixed. He emptied the rest of the water in the pitcher into an earthenware bowl, splashing it on his face and then using the end of a rough towel to scrub the dirt off his body. He was drying himself when there was a discreet knock on the doorframe. He turned to see Jacey Reynolds standing in the open doorway, smiling like a cat, the familiar briar pipe clenched between his teeth. Reynolds took the pipe out of his mouth with his right hand and waved it as a sort of greeting. He came into the room and sat down without ceremony.

'Colonel,' he said. 'Hear there's been trouble at the high country ranches.' Thompson just looked at him, his gaze flat and unbending. Reynolds gave a crooked grin.

'These are hard times,' he said.

'Don't give me that shit, Jace,' Thompson said. 'You weren't up there. It was . . . diabolical!'

'It was necessary,' Reynolds said abruptly, 'and you know it, so don't give me *that* shit, Brian!'

'I never knew . . .' began Thompson, all the force gone from his voice.

'. . . it would be like this?' jeered Reynolds. 'You want to play at the top table, soldier, you got to accept the stakes. If this deal goes through we'll all be in clover. And the Man got word from Washington: time is running out.'

'You mean they're going to . . .'

'Shut your mouth!' hissed Reynolds. 'Sometimes that loose mouth of yours worries me,' he went on, his voice resuming its normal sliding cadences. 'Rule one: we don't ever mention what we know, right?'

Thompson nodded dumbly.

'We have to control that land. There was no other way,' Reynolds said. He spread his hands. 'Regrettable, but . . .' he let the words drift away. 'Now we have another problem.'

Thompson sighed. He went to the bureau and pulled out a clean shirt, pulling it over his head.

'Larkin,' Reynolds said. Thompson froze, his arms in the

air, standing like a fond father trying to frighten a child by playing bugaboo. He poked his face through the collar opening.

'Larkin?' he squeaked.

'The Man said he knows too much,' Reynolds said. His voice was very mild. He puffed on the pipe contentedly.

'Then maybe he ought to come up here and take care of it himself,' railed Thompson. 'He . . .'

'. . . he'd take it badly if he knew you felt that way, Brian,' Reynolds interrupted, his voice as mild as ever. 'You've done very nicely out of all this.' He waved his arm to encompass the environs of the fort. 'A nice rakeoff on the trading at the store. Plenty of cheap liquor. And don't forget those IOUs of yours . . .'

'I'll pay them off, damn you,' ground out Thompson. 'A man'd go crazy up here unless he could do something.'

Reynolds held up a thin hand. 'I'm not sayin' you shouldn't play cards, Brian,' he remonstrated gently. 'Just reminding you that you owe us the best part of a thousand dollars. Now if that was to be brought to the attention of some people in Washington that the Man knows . . .'

'All right, damn you!' growled Thompson, shaking his head angrily like a roped steer. 'All right!'

'That's better,' Reynolds said. 'Now look. It's as easy as stealing candy from kids. Larkin is going to make a break for it.'

'He can't . . .' began Thompson.

'Listen to me!' snapped Reynolds, his indolence falling away. 'You just do like I say and everything will be sweet and easy. I already found out that you gave orders Larkin was to be shot on sight if he tried to escape. Well . . .' he grinned evilly. 'Doesn't that suggest anything to you?'

'You mean. . . ?'

'*Ley del fuego,*' nodded Reynolds. 'You got it in one. That tame boy-soldier of yours . . . what's his name?'

'Ellis,' Thompson replied.

'He's been in on this, hasn't he?'

'You know he has. He's bled me white.'

Reynolds smiled. 'I know. You've been very foolish, Brian.'

He steepled his fingers, leaning back in the armchair and smiling.

'All he has to do is get a gun to Larkin,' he said. 'He can do that, can't he?'

'I suppose so . . .' said Thompson reluctantly.

'Well, then,' Reynolds said, spreading his hands again. 'That's all there is to it.' He got up from the chair and walked towards the door. 'Don't botch it, Colonel,' he said, warningly. 'That could be . . . fatal.'

Thompson glared at his retreating back, and when Reynolds was gone, he slammed the drawer of the bureau shut with a savage gesture. He let his eyes roam restlessly around the cramped room, counting up mentally the pitifully few things in it which were his personal belongings.

'Forty years,' he muttered. 'For what?'

His eyes fell on the framed portrait which stood on the small table at the side of his bed. It showed a group of cadets in West Point uniforms, all smiling bravely at the camera, their youthful faces full of the future. The Class of '39. He picked the photograph up and laid it face down. Then he went to the door and sent his orderly to fetch Lieutenant Ellis.

CHAPTER NINETEEN

Angel cut Willy Mill's trail as the dawn broke brightly across the desert. Mill was traveling faster, as if he had decided he was clear and there was no need of concealment. One horse, one mule. So Mill probably still had the girl with him. Angel did not dare let his thoughts dwell upon her treatment at the hands of the raiders: every time the idea touched the edge of his mind a white anger welled in him. He knew he had to keep it under control. He wanted Mill alive.

Another thought struck him as he moved on at a steady

pace along the faint trace his quarry had left. Mill's interest in the girl had puzzled him. He was not the type. Mill would have killed her out of hand when the others were done with her. The man was totally devoid of normality and now the thought came to Angel that Mill would probably look upon her as a possession, something he could use to trade. In Tucson there was a market for women, particularly Anglo women, especially blonde Anglo women. Shipped across the border at Nogales, they were the symbols of wealth and status to the Mexican bandits who bought them for their pleasure, used them until they tired of them, and then put them into brothels for the miners and the gun runners and the black-hearted breed who infested the border. The thought made it harder for Angel to keep the horse at a steady pace, but he knew that if he pressed the animal now, it would founder. He had already mistreated it badly, but the dun was a sturdy beast. Too much more, and he would be afoot in the desert. He had to plan his strategy. He could not ride boldly into Tucson looking for Mill. There were too many places in a town a man could hole up, and he had no way of knowing what allies the man had there. Angel was a man not afraid of long odds, but he liked to know what they were. There was a proverb: a cautious man is one to cross bridges with. But the rage still seethed below his calm exterior. He still wanted a chance to kill Willy Mill. Very slowly, he told himself.

He reached the outskirts of Tucson late in the afternoon. The old walled town still looked pretty much the way it had been when the Spaniards had first passed this way. From a distance, they would hardly know it had changed, he thought. But along River Road the place was a straggle of honkytonks, cheap saloons, one or two lace-curtained, dark-windowed sporting houses with gingerbread woodwork on the verandas. Angel scanned the street. He saw no face he knew. He led the horse up to a barn-like building with a sign swinging over the door that said *livery stable* with no capital letters. It had bullet holes all around and over and under the letter 'i'. Inside, he found a lanky man sitting on a barrel, a bottle of beer in his hand.

'Like to bed the horse down for the night,' Angel said. 'He's been hard used.' The man cast an experienced eye over the animal and nodded.

'Ahuh,' the man said.

'Like to get him rubbed down, watered and grain fed,' Angel said. 'Can you handle that?'

'Ain't too busy,' the man said. 'Got but two or three hosses in. An' a mule.'

Angel's head came up. Could he have been that lucky?

'Been here long?' he asked idly.

This time the man's eyes came up to meet Angel's. They were cunning and bright and a leer edged its way towards the hostler's thin lips.

'I forget,' he said, craftily. Angel nodded, and pulled a ten-dollar gold piece from his watch pocket. He tossed it idly in the air. The foxy eyes followed it like a rat watching a day-old chick.

'How's your memory coming along?' Angel asked.

'Improvin' by the second,' the man said. He caught the gold coin deftly.

'Fat feller,' he said. 'Had some trollop with him.'

'Go on,' Angel said.

'Damned if I ain't gettin' a forgetful ol' fool,' the hostler said. The bright eyes were awash with greed.

'Damned if I don't agree,' said Angel. He reached forward and pulled the man to his feet, bunching the thin cotton shirt in his fist. He lifted the hostler until the man's feet were almost off the ground. The shifty eyes were a foot from his own, and the man squirmed like an eel.

'Hey,' he said, 'hey, there.'

'Ten bucks,' Angel reminded him. 'You want to have me take the small change out of your face?'

'Let go o' me, mister,' squealed the man. 'Ain't no call to git all riled up.'

Angel let him down with a thump. 'Talk!' he said. His eyes were that pale shade of grey and the man looked into them and gulped, his prominent Adam's apple jumping in his scrawny throat.

'Fat feller, like I said,' he managed. He spoke backing away from Angel until a safe distance separated them. 'Figgered he was a flesh peddler. With the girl an' all. We get lots of 'em,' he said, ingratiatingly. 'You need a piece?'

'You know a good place, I'm betting,' Angel said, disgust rising in his mouth.

'You're damn right I do. Same place that feller went,' the hostler said anxiously. 'I'll show it to you if you like.'

'Just tell me,' Angel said. 'They see you, I mightn't get in.'

The hostler frowned and then decided against letting his face reveal any reaction to the slur. This one was not for fooling around with, he told himself.

'Angela's, they call it,' he said. 'Account of it's run by this . . . lady.'

'She's Anglo,' he added, as if that made a subtle difference. 'Your friend was headed there.'

'Skip the testimonials,' Angel said sharply. 'Where is it?'

The man went to the doorway and pointed down the street.

'See thar where the road curves off to the right?' he said. 'It's a big ol' place, looks like it's some society lady owns it. Got red shingles on the roof.'

'How long ago did . . . my friend leave?'

'Hell, stranger, I don't rightly recall. . . .' He jumped as Angel turned and held up a placating hand. 'No, Jesus, mister, I was . . . it's just a way o' talkin'. Lemme see, he was here about, oh, an hour, hour an' a half ago. Not more.'

'You take real good care of that horse,' Angel said. '*Sabe?*'

'I'll treat him like he was my own brother,' the man said fervently.

'God help him,' Angel said, setting off down River Road. The bend was no more than a hundred yards away. He came around it, crossing the street to utilize the shelter of a lumbering team being cursed through the hock deep sand towards the Tanque Verde road. On this side of the street, he saw, there were stores, small, rundown, catering only for the drifters who congregated in River Road's sleazy saloons. The big house opposite was incongruously well kept. The windows were

114

cleaned and bright, the shutters painted and their hinges
oiled. There was a fine brass knocker on the black oak door.
The house had three stories. Angel paced on down the street,
and found a barber shop. He went inside. He could see the
entrance to the house quite easily from the barber's chair. He
longed for a bath, but it would have to wait. He told the barber
to shave him. On request, the barber sent out for a pitcher of
beer and a hunk of bread and cheese. Angel wolfed down the
food. The cheese was old but the bread was reasonably fresh.
He sank half of the pitcher of beer in a long and delicious
series of swallows. It tasted like cool, clear honey.

'Is there a doctor around here?' he asked the barber.

'Up on Elm,' the man said. 'If you want the fancy sort o'
doctorin'.'

'If not?'

'If it ain't something needs cuttin' or stitchin' I could
prob'ly do her,' the barber said. 'Old barber-shop custom, you
know. That's why we got them red an' white poles: bandages
an' blood, they represent. In the olden days, they . . .'

His voice faded away as Angel stripped off the filthy shirt
and revealed the sorry mess of bandages around his middle.

'Let's take a look at that there,' the barber said. He
unwound the bandage with surprisingly gentle fingers,
whistling when he saw what lay beneath.

'That looks right nasty,' he ventured. 'But it just needs
cleanin' up, I reckon. Ain't gone gangrene, far as I can tell.'

'Well, thanks a bundle,' Angel said.

The barber swabbed the puckered bullet wound with alcohol and painted iodine stripes all over the gravel scratches on
Angel's chest and forearms. Then he stood back to admire his
handiwork.

'I ain't about to ask you how all that happened,' he said,
'but you ought to be takin' it easy for a week or so.'

'I don't have the time,' Angel said. 'Can you put a bandage
or something on good and tight? Makes it easier to ride.'

'Ride? You could open that thing up like the Grand Canyon,
you start ridin', cowboy. What's up? Don't your outfit pay you

if you don't work?'

'I never asked. Get going with that bandaging, will you?'

The barber shook his head as he set about his task. 'Durn fool saddletramps,' he muttered. 'Walkin' around full o' holes, but will they do what the doc says, will they. . . ?'

He tucked in the end of the cotton bandage, and patted it affectionately with the air of a proud craftsman.

'That feels good,' Angel told him. 'Ought to hold fine.'

'Cripes, cowboy,' the barber said, 'that must be some rough outfit you work for.'

Angel grinned. 'It is at that,' he said. He invited the barber to share the rest of his beer, sending the same small Mexican boy out for some more. Angel gave him the money to buy a shirt and when he had drunk about another pint of beer and put on the gaudy Mexican nightmare the boy brought back, he felt refreshed and strong again.

Five minutes later, Willy Mill came out of the door of the house across the way, his face flushed and flaccid, his walk languid. He started east on River Road heading back towards the livery stable.

Angel was right behind him.

CHAPTER TWENTY

Lieutenant Peter Ellis was proud of his Army uniform. His family was an old one and his father and his father's father had been soldiers. Unlike them, however, Lieutenant Ellis was vain, headstrong, and ambitious, a combination of personality defects which in another lieutenant named Bascom had, some years earlier, plunged the entire Territory into bloody war with Cochise's Chiricahuas. In Ellis, the flaws in his personality produced a different kind of weakness: he was a compulsive gambler, and the worse for his plunging belief in his own 'luck.' It was this predilection which had led him to associate himself with the men who played poker regularly at the Reynolds and Birch trading store just off the post. Ellis was deep in debt to the store, and deep in debt to the saloons in Reynolds' Addition, the hellhole up in the hills. The deeper in debt he got the more he gambled, and the more he gambled the deeper he got into debt. At first, he had worried, but Reynolds had soothed him, hinting that in return for some minor 'favours' he would write off part of the debt. It was then that Ellis had learned that his Commanding Officer was also in the clutches of the partnership, was also doing 'favors' for Birch and Reynolds. An alliance between Thompson and Ellis had become a necessity, two weak men supporting each other's vanities, observing certain proprieties of conduct before the enlisted men but each knowing the other as a tool of the Daranga men and their mysterious master. It had never before been like this, though, Ellis thought. The whole thing was a nightmare: Thompson had left him in no doubt as to what was expected of them. And in no doubt that he, Ellis, would have to execute this latest 'favour' on his own.

Ellis had agreed, but for his own reasons. Thompson was no spring chicken: the man was going to pieces. Birch and Reynolds had pull, through their connections in Washington, and if a man had pull there, a command could easily be arranged. There weren't too many career men keen to spend their declining years in the sun-scoured discomfort of Fort Daranga. There were even fewer young ones. Ellis saw visions of a situation where he would control 'extras' as came the way of the Commanding Officer at Fort Daranga. Then, when he had the power, he would make Birch and Reynolds dance to a different tune. By God, they would pay then. Meantime . . .

This and thoughts like it went through his head as he did his rounds accompanied by Sergeant Battle and two enlisted men. When they reached the guardhouse, he motioned the sergeant to open the door of Larkin's cell. The old soldier's eyebrows rose a fraction, but he did as he was bid, pushing the door open and going in ahead of Ellis.

'On your feet, boy,' he said. The gunman spat on the floor.

117

Moving with a speed surprising in one so bulky, Battle crossed the cell and pulled Larkin off the cot, jamming him against the rough wall, slamming the breath from the man's body.

'That's a good boy,' Battle said. He wasn't even breathing heavily. Larkin just looked at the sergeant with hooded eyes. Ellis came in.

'At ease, Sergeant,' he said. 'I want to talk to the prisoner.'

Sergeant Battle stepped back.

'Alone,' Ellis said meaningfully. Battle frowned and turned, hesitating at the door. His eyes touched the holstered revolver at the lieutenant's belt. Ellis caught the glance and smiled.

'You're right, of course,' he said, letting the words come out as if they might rot his teeth. He unbuckled the belt and handed it to the sergeant, who went out of the cell.

'What the hell do you want?' Larkin rasped.

'A quiet talk, that's all,' Ellis said, sitting down on the hard cot. 'Take it easy.'

'You try takin' it easy when you've been cooped up in this sweatbox as long as me,' snapped Larkin.

'Easy,' Ellis told him sibilantly. He held up a warning hand and rose, going to the judas window in the cell door. Through it he could see the sergeant talking to one of the two guards. He turned and sat down again, his voice dropping conspiratorially.

'You want out,' he said, 'so out you're going. It's on.'

Larkin's eyes lifted, comprehension dawning in them.

'Jesus,' he said. 'He thinks of everything.' He looked long and hard at the young soldier. 'So you're on the payroll too?'

'Never mind that,' Ellis said. There was irritation in his voice at the thought that Larkin was classing him as an equal because they both helped the same people. It was like a raw Irish recruit imagining himself the equal of a general.

'Shut your dirty mouth,' he snapped, 'and be thankful that you have friends like Jacey Reynolds to look after you.'

'Dirty, is it,' Larkin grinned. 'A spade is a spade, sonny.'

'I told you to shut up,' ground out Ellis. 'If I had my way

you'd rot in here till hell froze, you cheap thug.'

Larkin's eyes narrowed, but he let the insult pass. If he had to suffer a fool to get out of this, he had to suffer and that was that. Larkin was not a man to try changing the opinions of a pigheaded little ass-kisser like this one.

'Get on with it,' he said. 'How do we work it?'

'It's all as simple as this,' Ellis said. He unbuttoned his shirt and pulled out an Army Colt. Larkin grabbed it, checking the loads, hefting the weapon. His eyes glowed with a pale light; he looked like a different man with the gun in his hand.

'What's the drill?' he said, softly.

'There's to be no shooting,' Ellis told him. 'That's imperative. There should be no need to use . . . that. When the guards bring in your grub, you make your move. Knock them out, tie them up, anything you like. But no shooting – you understand? I can't help you if there's any shooting. It would be heard all over the Fort!'

'Damn you for a fool, I can see that,' Larkin said. 'How do I get away?'

'After retreat, I'll bring a horse round in back,' Ellis said. 'It will be tethered behind the guardhouse in the yard. All you have to do is get on it and disappear.'

Larkin nodded. 'Better get me a carbine,' he said. 'Leave it in the saddle holster.'

'I'll do what I can,' Ellis said stiffly. 'They don't hang from the trees waiting to be picked, you know.'

'Get one,' Larkin hissed. 'Just get one.'

The venom in his voice made Ellis recoil, a stirring of fear touching the nape of his neck. The man was an animal, he told himself. He stilled the reaction; after all, Larkin would be dead in a few hours. The thought of his part in that made his hands tremble for a moment. He wiped the sweat off them on his pants.

'Did you . . . those men: Clare, and the old man. Were you sent. . . ?'

'Now that'd be tellin', wouldn't it?' grinned Larkin. His teeth shone whitely in the shadowy cell.

Ellis's curiosity got the better of him. 'Why are they doing all this? The attack on the high country ranches ... what's behind it all, Larkin?'

'If I knew I wouldn't tell you, sonny,' Larkin said. 'Just do what the Man tells you an' don't ask questions. You'll live longer.'

The peculiar aptness of the remark made Ellis start guiltily, but Larkin was not looking at him.

'I don't know what you're talkin' about, Lieutenant,' he said loudly. 'Why don't you go 'way an' leave me alone?'

Ellis followed the direction of Larkin's gaze and saw Sergeant Battle's eyes peering through the Judas window.

'Very well,' he said heavily, picking up the cue and rising from the cot.

'You've had your chance, Larkin.'

'Ah, go to hell,' Larkin snapped. He slouched down on the vacated cot and Ellis waved for the sergeant to open the door.

'Hopeless,' he remarked. The sergeant said nothing. They went into the outer room and the two guards there came to attention and saluted as they left the guardhouse. Then when the officer was gone they went back to their game of poker.

'Officers,' said one.

'Shut up and deal,' said the other.

The last muted sounds of the bugle blowing retreat had faded, and the flag had been furled and put in its canvas sack. Lights were coming on here and there in the buildings around the Fort. The sky was streaked with purple and black. In the bunk-houses the men who had been at the raided ranches told ever-gorier anecdotes of what they had found and what they had seen to their open-mouthed comrades who had remained on the post.

In the guardhouse, the two soldiers on duty brought Larkin his food. One of them unlocked the padlock and stood back, rifle canted casually while the other came into the cell with the tray of food for the prisoner. At the beginning they had done this warily, watching Larkin like hawks, but he had totally ignored them, sitting slouched on his cot as he was doing now, his head turned away. Neither man was expecting tonight to be any different; they were thinking of the game they had broken off to bring Larkin his grub.

Larkin came off the cot like a tiger, his long arm wrapping around the neck of the guard bending to put down the tray, cutting off his wind and preventing any outcry. He bent the man backwards like a bow, even as the other guard opened his mouth, the rifle coming level, unsure whether to shout out or to fire the rifle and in his moment of hesitation, Larkin let the guard see the gun.

'Freeze!' he hissed. The soldier froze. 'Drop the rifle ... easy!' The Spencer clattered to the floor and as it did, Larkin released the guard he had been throttling, letting the man slump to his knees. Larkin smashed him to the floor with a sweeping blow from the gun barrel. The man went down flat without a whimper. Larkin stepped over the guard's body and jammed the gun into the belly of the gaping boy in the corridor.

'Move,' he snapped, herding the guard into the outer room, picking up the Spencer as he did. Through the window Larkin could see the parade ground: it lay silent and empty. He told the young guard to turn around and the boy half turned away, his fear evident, trying to see Larkin out of the corner of his eye, trying to summon the courage to shout. Larkin hit him very hard just above the ear with the barrel of the gun, and again as the boy fell to his knees. The soldier measured his length on the packed dirt floor, his legs kicking slightly. Blood dribbled from the open mouth. Then Larkin went to the door, opening it a few inches, a foot wide. Nothing. He grabbed a handful of shells for the Spencer from an ammunition pouch hanging on a wall peg, and stuffed them in his pocket. His mouth was drawn wide in a snarling grin as he eased through the open door, hugging the wall of the guardhouse like a shadow, sliding along its face and into the dark of the alley between the guardhouse and a long low building which stood opposite.

The alley was as black as the cellars of hell and Larkin moved carefully, testing the ground with each foot before putting his weight on it. Behind the guardhouse was an open yard, with a low adobe wall about ten yards away. Beyond it was the open plain.

Larkin rounded the corner of the building and stood stock still in the shadow. There was no sign of a horse behind the guardhouse. He swore silently. That puffed-up idiot of a boy lieutenant! He slid around the corner, in case the horse was at the far side. Nothing. A touch of coolness, something in the air, a feeling coming from the far side of nowhere touched the nape of his neck, insidious and chilling. As the thought formed in his mind he saw a figure rise behind the adobe wall, pistol in hand.

'Corporal of the Guard!' the man yelled. 'Corporal of the Guard – prisoner escaping!' Ellis! Larkin threw himself backwards into the sand as the lieutenant fired a shot which whacked a hunk of adobe out of the wall of the guardhouse. Larkin swarmed to his feet, finding the wall on the far side of the alley, hearing Ellis fire the gun again, probably into the air, no bullet came, Larkin swift-footing behind the long building, crouched down so that his body did not show black against the white frames of the windows set at shoulder height in the wall. He heard hoarse shouts as men turned out in response to the shouts and the firing, running feet crunching on the gravel of the parade ground.

He saw figures coming into the open from the darkness of the alley he had just vacated and went down on one knee, aiming the Spencer, letting the flat hard sound of the rifle drive them diving for cover like prairie dogs touched by the shadow of a hawk, and levered another shell into the breech, looking for a target, looking for escape simultaneously, running, crouched, another twenty yards, out away from the building as someone by the guardhouse turned loose with a sixgun. Hoarse commands, and the firing stopped. He heard someone shout.

'Can you see him, sir?' It was the big sergeant.

Larkin pulled the Army Colt from his belt and fired three shots at the windows of the long building – a bunkhouse, enlisted men's quarters? The shattering glass brought oaths and the sound of running feet, and he could vaguely see bulky shapes on the ground crawling rapidly towards the spot at which he had fired. He was already running, but this time across the path of his pursuers like a banderillero quartering across the path of the bull, heading for the wall behind the guardhouse. More men were pouring into the yard now and he saw Ellis running long-legged across the guardhouse yard and he smiled. If he died for it. . . . The sixgun, laid across Larkin's forearm for steadiness, spoke abruptly and Ellis faltered in mid-stride, as if he had tripped on something. He went on running but he was going sideways and down and he reeled into the dirt face first, legs kicking high in agony.

Larkin scuttled to the far end of the wall, and heard Sergeant Battle shout an order which brought all the men to their feet, running hard at the wall where he had been, and as they moved, Larkin moved in the opposite direction, close to the ground, shielded by the purple night, back to the wall of the guardhouse and out into the open without thought when he saw a soldier come flailing up the alley on horseback, bearing down on the knotted men ahead. Larkin fired the Spencer from the hip as the soldier came into the yard and the man cartwheeled out of the saddle, and then Larkin was in the saddle. He threw the rifle at a man who reached up for him, rode another man down. He fired the rest of the bullets in the Army Colt into the stricken faces ahead and then he was past them and around the end of the adobe wall, hearing the shouts behind him and the flat boom of rifles. Slugs zipped angrily in the air, lost in the rushing wind as Larkin rode flat out into the darkness, fading into the night, four dead and two wounded on the ground in the yard of the guard-house.

CHAPTER TWENTY-ONE

Mill got his horse from the livery stable and rode out of town. A mile or two along the old Spanish Trail he stopped at a hacienda. It was a rambling, colonial style of house, with a pillared portico and one of those iron jockeys with a ring in his hand next to a mounting stone such as were popular back east in the big Virginia mansions. From the shelter of a stand of scrub oak, Angel watched the man tie his horse to the iron ring and after a moment, go in. Angel tethered the dun to one of the trees and using such cover as he could find, worked his way close to the house. There was a white board fence, warped a little by the sun, and grass had been planted in front of the house. He eased over the fence, taking up a position behind a big cottonwood which shaded the house.

The man who came behind him must have been specially trained, for he was a big man. The grass muffled his approach, and Angel was much too late to act when he heard the last movement. The sound of a hammer being eased back froze him, and he held his hands away from the gun at his side. 'That's good, suh,' the voice said. Angel turned to see a huge black man standing in the sunlight, a brand new Winchester carbine leveled at him. The man jerked the barrel of the gun, indicating that Angel should walk towards the house. When he reached the porch the Negro stayed at the foot of the steps. Another much older Negro opened the door, and inside Angel saw Willy Mill smiling at him flatly. Standing next to Mill was a well-built man with a shock of white hair crowning a leonine head. His smile of welcome was warm and friendly, the keen blue eyes bright in a maze of laughter wrinkles. The shock of recognition must have showed on Angel's face, for the man laughed out loud.

'I see you know me, Mr Angel,' he said. 'Come in, come in.'

'Senator,' Angel acknowledged.

The man shook his head. 'You are a foolish man, Mr Angel,' he said, a trace of sadness in his voice. 'I had hoped this would not happen.'

'I can imagine,' Angel said drily. 'Senator Ludlow Burnstine of Arizona: employing a psychopathic killer isn't quite the image you've been trying to give people in Washington.'

Burnstine shook his head again, as though at the folly of mankind. His clothes were unobtrusive but obviously expensive, well cut. He wore them like a man who needs to give no thought to his appearance. His calf boots glowed with the sheen that only long and diligent polishing can impart to leather. The politician's face was tanned, handsome. A real actor, thought Angel. Burnstine was a popular figure in Washington, his Georgetown house an oasis of good food, good wine, and the top-drawer of Washington society. His reputation as a *bon-vivant* was complemented by the healthy respect accorded him by his political enemies. Ludlow Burnstine was a powerful man and the revelation of his involvement in the affairs of Daranga was shocking in a way. The man certainly didn't need money, Angel thought. The high-ceilinged hallway in which they stood was tiled with intricately patterned Moorish tiles. Plants flourished in the greenhouse atmosphere created by tinted windows let into the ceiling. Somewhere Angel could hear the soft sound of a fountain playing.

'Shall we go inside?' Burnstine said, gesturing to the doorway on the left, every bit the gracious host with the unexpected caller. They went into a fine, masculine room, warm with oak paneling, the big desk topped with gold-tooled leather that looked Florentine. There were shelves packed with richly bound books on one side of the room. The floor was carpeted, heavy drapes shaded the windows. Angel whistled through his teeth.

'You sure do have it nice, Senator,' he observed. 'What you're doing doesn't make sense.'

'Oh, come now, Mr Angel,' Burnstine said. 'Let us not argue before we know each other. William, a chair for Mr Angel.' Mill growled an oath, but Burnstine just looked at him, and the fat man grudgingly pushed a fat winged-arm chair an inch towards Angel.

'Let me offer you a drink,' Burnstine said, waving an arm towards a trolley on which was arrayed a glittering selection of cut glass decanters and glasses.

'Whiskey, perhaps? Or bourbon? Name it, I'm sure we can take care of you.' He smiled, docking his head at his own words. 'That's rather good, I must say.'

'Lovely,' Angel said. 'Whiskey is fine.'

Burnstine nodded, the nod of a man approving the judg-ment of an inferior, and poured a healthy measure into one of the crystal glasses.

'Eight years old,' he said proudly, handing the glass over. 'I have it freighted here from San Francisco. Twenty dollars a bottle and worth every cent of it.'

Angel sipped the drink. It was a pleasant change from Arizona rotgut and he said so. Burnstine flinched at this lapse of taste.

'When you get to my time of life, you appreciate the finer things,' he said.

'None of us is getting any younger,' he added, his smile as mellow as brandy.

'I'm impressed, I'm impressed,' Angel said. 'Now, do you want to tell me what this' – he jerked a thumb at the fat man slumped in his chair pouring the fine brandy he had poured for himself down his gullet – 'is doing here?'

'Let us not mince words with each other, Mr Angel,' Burnstine said. 'Do not attempt to act the innocent with me. At least pay me the compliment of speaking truthfully.'

Angel nodded, and took another sip of the whiskey.

'OK,' he said. 'The murders at the high country ranches in Daranga were ordered by you, carried out by Boot and this one and a gang of mercenaries from – where, Grant County?'

'Very good, very good,' Burnstine said, smiling like a fond parent with a clever child.

'And Larkin?'

Burnstine smiled. 'Of course. Larkin, too.'

'Why?'

'It seemed better to present a mystery to the good people of Daranga. They could obviously not connect the killings to Boot and Mill, and so they would not by definition connect them to others . . . others which had happened.'

'Stupid,' Angel said flatly.

'Not stupid,' Burnstine said softly. 'I do not mind telling

you, Mr Angel, since I am sure you are aware that you will not live to repeat what I say. There was a time factor.'

'Go on.'

'All in good time. First you must tell me what your Department knows of events in Daranga.'

'Everything,' Angel said.

'I think not, my dear fellow. I am not without my own sources of information on Capitol Hill.'

'So I've heard.'

'It perturbs me only slightly that the Justice people have seen fit to meddle in my affairs. In Washington, your friend the Attorney General may wield a certain limited power. No more, perhaps, than a dozen others including myself. Here in Arizona, however, I am the law, all-powerful, all-seeing. Shall I tell you how powerful I am?'

'Could I stop you?'

Burnstine ignored the jibe. 'The barber who shaved you and shared your beer, the Mexican boy who ran your errands, the hostler whom you treated so cavalierly – all of them sent word, via various means, to me. I knew every step you took here in Tucson as I do every step that any man takes.'

'What about your flesh-peddler?'

Burnstine's lip curled with distaste.

'That is none of your concern, although William and I may have words about it later,' the old man said. Willy Mill shifted uneasily in the chair, reaching for the brandy again. 'But in the ultimate analysis, I am satisfied that what happened to the girl was for the best.'

'For you, or for her?'

'You are impertinent, Mr Angel, but you have a certain rough wit which I rather regret I shall not be able to cultivate. Let me remind you that you still live only because I permitted it.'

'You may be a little tin God down here in Tucson, Senator,' Angel said. 'But whatever you're up to, you won't get away with it. There are too many weak links.'

Burnstine reached behind him for a teak humidor, and

offered Angel a cigar. When Angel shook his head, the old man shrugged and took a silver cigar cutter from his vest pocket, trimming the end of the cigar, making a ceremony of lighting it.

'Pure Havana,' he said, inhaling the blue smoke. 'What weak links?' The old eyes were shrewd in their pouched, wrinkled lashless sockets.

'Larkin, for one,' Angel said. 'He's under arrest in Fort Daranga. When he goes for trial, he'll talk. He won't do twenty years in Yuma for you, Senator.'

'Larkin,' smiled Burnstine softly, 'Ah, yes.' He took a watch from a fob pocket.

'I would say Mr Larkin is probably being buried at Fort Daranga right now.'

'Buried?'

'*Ley del fuego*, I imagine they'll say,' Burnstine smiled. 'Killed while trying to escape.'

'Then I was right about that, too,' Angel said, his lips tight. 'Thompson is—'

'Of course,' Burnstine waved a hand. A diamond winked in the sunlight.

'Another weak link,' Angel pointed out.

'Bah,' snorted the old man. 'Thompson? The man's a wreck. Cards, liquor, women – when word of his personal proclivities reaches the right ears he'll be drummed out of the Army. Who'd believe the ravings of a court-martialed drunkard?'

Angel stuck grimly to his guns. 'You've been pushed into the open, man,' he said. 'If I disappear, if any more killings happen in the Rio Blanco country, the Department will move in on you in force. You'll be finished.'

Burnstine leaned forward. He jabbed with the cigar to emphasize his points as he spoke. 'Listen, Mr Angel' – jab – 'there will be no more trouble in the Rio Blanco country.' Jab. 'The Circle C and the Perry ranch will be sold to pay the mortgages, and I' – jab – 'I will own them.'

'I thought Birch and Reynolds owned all that land up there?'

'Nominally they do,' Burnstine said. 'But they have no resources of their own. Everything of theirs is mortgaged to the hilt – to me. They are merely – what is the phrase – men of straw, front men for me. That land is mine.'

'You ever going to tell me why it was worth killing so many people for?'

'But of course, my dear fellow,' Burnstine said, leaning back expansively.

'It would be most unfair to ask that you face your death without at least the satisfaction of knowing why you are dying.' He gestured again with the cigar, jabbing to emphasize his remarks. 'In two months' time, the Rio Blanco will be dammed at Twin Peaks. The high country will be partially flooded to make a huge irrigation reservoir, and the lower valley will become one of the most fertile pieces of land in the West. Imagine it! Orange trees, peach orchards! Huge tracts of farming land worth millions. The desert will bloom, Angel. Our bountiful Government is going to spend ten million dollars to make it bloom – for me!' His eyes glowed with an almost religious light. 'There are over two hundred thousand acres on the Reynolds place, nearly as much again on the Birch ranch. When the project is completed, land in the Rio Blanco valley will sell for fifty, a hundred dollars an acre. Think of it, man! Forty million dollars! Do you think I would let one man, ten men, a hundred stand in the way of that? I will be the richest man in the United States. In Washington, I will use that wealth to its greatest effect. I will sway the President, the Cabinet. This country will be mine to play with like a puppet!' He paused, letting the lambent light dim slightly in his eyes, regaining his self-control. Sweat was beading his brow. He let his breath out slowly.

'So, Mr Angel. I have told you this to show you my power. I doubt that your civil servant's mentality can grasp the immensity of what I have done, but you must now realize how futile your efforts to prevent my realizing my ambitions really were.'

'You know, of course, that you are insane,' Angel told him.

Burnstine lurched to his feet, and with a swift movement

came around the desk. He towered over the seated man, and drew back his hand. Angel awaited the blow impassively but it never came. Burnstine's hand dropped, and a smile touched his spittle-flecked lips.

'Ah, no,' he said, softly. 'No need of that at all.'

He leaned back against the desk.

'I have enjoyed our talk, Mr Angel,' he said. He picked up a golden bell and shook it. The door opened and a huge Negro came into the room.

'John,' Burnstine said. 'Mr Angel is leaving us.'

'Yessuh,' the man said.

'I'm coming along,' Mill said, getting to his feet. 'I want a part of this.'

Burnstine frowned. Then he smiled. 'Of course, William. You are entitled to your pleasures, too. Goodbye, Mr Angel.'

He turned around and went behind the desk, sitting down and taking another cigar from the teak humidor.

'Take him out and kill him,' he said and his voice rasped like a file on steel.

CHAPTER TWENTY-TWO

Metter had disobeyed Angel's instructions; but heading back now with the patrol towards Fort Daranga he did not think his friend would mind. Riding like the wind, he had pushed back towards the Rincons. The horse was a good one: Metter had raised him from a foal, and it had saddened him to use on such a fine animal the Apache tricks he had finally needed to employ to make it continue until he found the patrol led by Lieutenant Blackstone. The Apaches could make a horse abandoned by a white man get up and run another fifty miles. What they did to make the horse run was unpleasant but highly effective: Metter winced as he remembered the experience, but it had been necessary and it had worked. He had intercepted the patrol well back of the place where the raiders had turned away from Boot and Mill. A trooper had been detailed to ride one of the pack mules and with a fresh mount between his knees, Metter had piloted the patrol at a flat gallop up through the central pass of the Rincons, taking them on a line which formed the string to the bow of the raiders' trail. They had come down out of the hills as the raiders came around them, and in a running fight on the scrub-dotted malpais, the sixteen troopers had taken a savage and exultant revenge upon the men who had done the senseless killing in the high chaparral ranches. The mercenaries, outnumbered and with no stomach for a real fight, had tried to run for it, and the cavalrymen had cut them down without compassion. Of the dozen raiders, seven had been killed. One cavalryman was dead. The surviving raiders had been bound hand and foot, then a rope, noosed around each neck, had been linked between each of them and they were being led, none too gently, in single file back to face justice at Fort Daranga.

They arrived at the Fort in mid-morning to find it in turmoil. The raiders were shoved unceremoniously into the guardhouse, the men dismissed. They hurried to the bunkhouses to hear the story that Metter and Lieutenant Blackstone were being told at the same time by a tall, slender major who had arrived at the Fort only an hour before them. Major Patrick Janson was a member of the personal staff of the General of the Army, and his mission was to deliver orders to Colonel Brian Thompson which required his presence as a principal participant in a General Court Martial at Fort Leavenworth on charges of gross misconduct. Thompson had been two hours gone, leading the patrol south in pursuit of the fugitive Larkin, when Janson had arrived. The major was ensconced in the Commanding Officer's quarters, awaiting his return with some anticipation. There is nothing so universally detested by a professional soldier as the discovery that a brother officer and gentleman has abused the rank and privilege of his command. Major Janson had seen some of the evidence which was to be presented at the Court Martial, and it was damning. It consisted of documents showing payments of sums of money, IOUs, unpaid bills of substantial amounts for liquor, the scrawled affidavits of half a dozen men whose names were unknown to him. They had arrived by mail in a package postmarked from St Louis, Missouri, without any covering letter. Whoever the anonymous sender was, he had presented the United States Army with an open and shut case against Thompson. Janson was certain the man would be stripped of his rank, drummed out of the Service, discharged with complete ignominy. There had been another set of orders for Lieutenant Peter Burford Ellis. The discovery that Ellis had been killed the preceding night in an escape made by a prisoner from the guardhouse had to some extent been a relief to Janson. He took no pleasure from seeing the service in disrepute. Bury the man and the accusations, he thought: so much the better.

Some of this he told the two men: the part which concerned them. He told them about Larkin's break-out, the evidence of the guards that Larkin had a gun, the patrol of twenty-five men headed by Colonel Thompson which was pursuing the fleeing man. He told them who he was and where he was from. He did not tell them why he was in Fort Daranga, and was thankful that neither man asked.

'You think that Larkin's escape may have been an inside job?' Metter asked.

'It seems possible, at least,' Janson said. 'There is no doubt that he managed to get hold of a gun somehow.'

'Who had he talked to?'

'The guards say that Lieutenant Ellis spent some time in Larkin's cell questioning him. But' – he raised a hand – 'Ellis left his gun with Sergeant Battle. So we must not jump to any conclusions, gentlemen.'

'And Ellis is dead, so we can't ask him,' Blackstone mused.

Janson nodded. 'A little – ah, pat, perhaps,' he said. 'When Larkin is taken we shall find out.'

'He'll be hard to take,' Metter said. 'He rode south, you say?'

Janson nodded.

'Heading for Daranga, mebbe,' Metter continued. He turned to Blackstone. 'Can you let me have a hoss?'

'I think we can do that,' Blackstone said. 'When I tell the Major your part in taking those raiders, I'm sure he won't argue.'

'Give Mr Metter anything he needs,' Janson said crisply. 'Then perhaps you'd be kind enough to come back here, Lieutenant. I'd like to hear your version of the events of the last week – in detail.'

'Yes, sir!' Blackstone said, enthusiastically. He accompanied Metter outside and sent an orderly running to the stables to fetch a fresh mount. He smacked a fist into the palm of his hand.

'God, Metter!' he said, 'I'd forgotten what real officers were like.'

'I know what you mean,' Metter replied. 'I'd say things are going to be right lively at Fort Daranga.'

'And about time,' Blackstone said, 'about time!'

Metter swung into the saddle. He patted the canteen of water lovingly. 'I'll drink that before I've gone a mile,' he grinned.

'Good luck, Metter,' Blackstone said, his face going serious. 'If you see Angel, tell him we evened the score, won't you?'

'I'll tell him,' Metter said, and touched the spurs to the horse's side. Frisky from the stables, the bay moved off at a steady lope. Metter neck-reined it around to the south, and headed out towards Daranga.

*

'This'll do. Get down, Angel.'

Mill's voice was silky. They were perhaps three miles out of Tucson, but they might well have been a hundred. They were in a narrow defile, the weather-scoured rocks relieved only in a few places by scattered clumps of brush which clung precariously where an earth-filled crevice gave them root-hold, huge rocks and thickets the only breaks in the dun contours. The stillness of the place closed in on them, and the blazing sun hung in a vault of brazen white, its heat tangible. Nothing moved. No lizard scuttled, no jackrabbit loped between bushes. It was as if death lived in the place, enforcing on the natural life an unnatural stillness, the quiet of the grave.

Mill's command was almost a relief. Through the miles they had ridden, Angel had felt a crawling tension ever-present between his shoulder-blades. They could have shot him anywhere, at any time. All through the journey the Negro had not spoken once. Now he had dismounted and was unstrapping a folding shovel, such as the Army carried on field expeditions, from the saddle.

'Get down, I said!' Mill's command was repeated and this time emphasized by a gesture from the gleaming carbine canted across his chunky thighs.

Angel shrugged, lifting his leg over the saddlehorn and sliding down to the ground effortlessly, in spite of his bound hands. The Negro dropped the shovel to the ground and came around both men in a wide half circle, taking no chances of getting between them. He produced a wicked-looking folding knife which sliced through the ropes binding Angel's hands like butter. Angel stood rubbing his forearms to get the circulation moving again as the Negro stepped back, and unhurriedly as ever unhitched a sawn-off Greener shotgun from the pommel of his saddle, where it hung from a rawhide loop. He covered Angel as Mill dismounted.

Mill kicked the shovel towards Angel.

'Dig,' he said.

'You mind if I get my blood moving first?' Angel asked.

'Diggin'll do it,' Mill said. 'Quit stallin'.'

'If you're planning to cut me down anyway, I'd just as soon not bother,' Angel told him.

'I don't mind persuadin' you some,' Mill said. An evil light kindled his eyes, as the idea threaded into the sick part of his brain. He reached up on his saddle and uncoiled a braided rope. The Negro watched.

'The Senator he din say nothin' about whuppin' him,' he said mildly.

'He didn't say nothin' about not whippin' him, neither,' Mill said. 'Just keep that thing pointed at him. Move over to one side a bit, while I see if I can't get him to co-operate.' He let the reata whistle through the air as he swung it. He flicked it at Angel's face, and Angel flinched backwards. The rope whistled back as Mill flicked it, and the rough braids whipped a welt on Angel's cheek.

'Purty,' hissed Mill. He licked his thick lips, his breath coming heavily.

Again he looped the rope, again flicking it out like the striking tongue of a snake. Angel stepped back, stumbling over a rock. Before he could regain his balance, Mill struck. The rope flayed across Angel's back, ripping his shirt. Specks of blood tinged the cotton, spotting the gay Mexican colors.

'Lovely,' Mill muttered.

Angel looked at the other man. 'You going to let him do this?' he shouted. 'Can't you see he's sick? Look at him – he's sick inside! He's enjoying it, it's giving him a thrill!'

The big eyes flickered in the dark face, and then went studiously blank. He said nothing as Mill again twirled the rope.

'Sick, am I?' Mill grinned. His lips were wet and loose, and sweat patches darkened his shirt. 'How's that for sick, my purty boy?' Again the whistle of the rope; this time Angel dodged it.

'Stand still, damn you!' screamed Mill. 'Make him stand still, you stupid idiot!'

There was a demented look in the piggy eyes. His fat thighs were shaking with some inner excitement. He caressed the rope as it passed through his chubby hands, crooning to it.

'Lovely, lovely,' he said. 'Lovely.'

'I reckon that's enough, mister,' the other man said. 'Why don't we-all jest kill him now?'

'In a moment, in a moment,' Mill hissed. He was coiling the rope again. Angel played his last card.

'Did I tell you how Johnny died, Willy?' he said. Mill looked

135

up, something slipping behind his eyes, a strange wild uniden-
tifiable flicker on the near side of total madness.

'You,' he screamed, his voice high-pitched, womanlike.
'You! Killed! *Johnny*?'

'I shot his damned head off,' Angel said, hurling the words
brutally at Mill like a challenge. Mill heard them and Angel
could see the things behind his eyes working on the picture
the words had formed, and then the light went out and Mill
gave a shrill screech that went up and up and up and he
launched himself at the man in front of him. The Negro
jerked backwards, almost pulling the triggers of the Greener,
but he stopped just in time to avoid blowing Mill apart and in
that same second Angel was moving forward in hard and fast,
flinging himself into the reaching fingers of the demented
Mill, who reacted as Angel had hoped he would, clawing at
Angel's face like a woman, sobbing incomprehensible phrases,
his body between Angel and the tall man.

'Leggo, mister!' shouted the Negro, dancing off to one side
and then back, trying to get a clear shot at Angel. 'Leggo of
him!'

He might as well have shouted the words to a tiger at the kill.
Mill's clawing fingers were trying to reach Angel's throat, and he
was kicking and spitting, his weight bearing the lighter man backwards.

The Negro let one of the barrels of the shotgun go into the
ground, the explosion penetrating Mill's crazed mind. His grip
loosened momentarily and in that moment Angel flicked the
gun from the holster at Mill's side, straight-arming the fat man
away from him and bringing the sixgun into deadly unerring
action in one blur of movement.

The Negro was good, very good. He saw the movement, read
it, was moving to the side even as Angel fired, but Angel had
fired his three shots knowing that the man would move and the
first slug hit the Negro high in the chest, on the right side, the
second in the neck, tearing out the larynx and the soft muscles
of the throat. The third hit him just below the nose. The
combined force of the impact drove the man over backwards

dead on his feet as Angel hit the ground and the Negro's fingers tightened involuntarily on the triggers of the sawn-off Greener. The huge *zzboooomf!* as the gun went off shocked the silence of the badlands and the wicked, tearing, close-grouped shot hit Mill just above the base of his spine, all of them in a space that could have been covered by a man's hand, bursting through him in a terrible red welter of spraying tissue, hurling the fat man sideways in a tattered heap. Mill lay screaming, his eyes wide open, the middle of his body a nightmare. He scrambled around on the ground, biting through his lips in agony, his eyes sightless with pain. Angel picked himself up warily, the .45 cocked and ready in his hand, although he knew he would not need it. He went over to Mill. The screaming had stopped now, and Angel knew the man had bitten his tongue so badly that it had swollen to fill the whole mouth. Mill looked at Angel. The sickness was still there, far back, behind the agony. Angel shook his head.

'You can hear me, Willy,' he said. A sound came from the thing on the ground. It might have been assent, or a plea for something else.

'I wanted you alive, Willy,' Angel said. 'I wanted you to hang. Maybe this way is better. This way you pay the full price: for Freeman, and MacIntyre, Stevens, all those men you killed up in the high country. And for the girl, Willy. Especially for the girl.'

He slung the shotgun on to the pommel of the saddle and tied the reins of the horses together, holding them as he mounted his own dun. He looped the reins around the pommel and moved the horse away from where the fat man lay, with eyes imploring, begging, and the throat working to make a sound, a plea. Angel moved the horse down the defile and headed for the open plain. He kept his mind resolutely closed to what would happen to the fat man back in the defile, and he did it with complete success until he was about a quarter of a mile away. Then he heard Mill scream. It was a wild and awful sound, totally insane, a sound that bounced off the canyon walls and echoed into the deepest recesses of Angel's consciousness. The scream went on, a sound of purest animal terror and the scream was a word and the word, long, drawn-out, and terrible, was 'No!'

Angel shook the reins and the horse moved into a lope, heading west. Behind him the buzzards floated down gently on the rising hot air, easing down towards the grisly thing below. Angel did not look back.

CHAPTER TWENTY-THREE

Angel reached Tucson under cover of darkness. He made no attempt to conceal himself. Burnstine expected him to be dead – and buried, he thought grimly – and nobody here knew him by sight except Burnstine's Negro servants. He kept a sharp eye for any black face along the busy sidewalks, but saw few black people. An old woman walking proudly upright beneath an enormous bundle of washing directed him to the office of the United States marshal on Elm Street. The marshal, John Allan, was a tall, slim, fair-haired man who listened with growing amazement to the story Angel told him.

'By God!' he would growl, every once in a while, 'By God!' And he would hit his knee with a clenched fist. When Angel finished his story, Allan wasted no more time. Within half an hour he had rounded up half a dozen men whom he told Angel were completely reliable, and within another fifteen minutes they were hammering on the door of Burnstine's hacienda.

After a few minutes a light came on in the hall and the same Negro who had opened it to Angel before swung the door wide. He fell back several steps as Angel stuck a six-gun under his nose, his eyes as wide as saucers with fear and surprise.

'Quick, now,' snapped Angel. 'Is Burnstine here?'

The Negro shook his head. His lips trembled and when he

tried to speak his teeth chattered. Allan touched Angel's arm, his eyes indicating that Angel should put away the gun. He spoke to the terrified servant in a gentle voice.

'What's your name, boy?' he said, ignoring the fact that the Negro was old enough to be his father, perhaps even his grand-father.

'Gee, suh,' the Negro managed, gulping. 'Banner Gee.'

'Well, Banner, we ain't going to hurt you none,' Allan said. 'You know me?'

'Yassuh,' Gee said. 'Yo're the marshal.'

'And you know I work for the Government, Banner,' Allan continued softly. The Negro nodded. 'So does this gentleman here, Banner,' Allan went on. 'He's not goin' to hurt you none.'

'Yassuh.' The Negro nodded, his eyes losing their startled whiteness.

'The senator is in bad trouble, Banner,' Allan said. His voice was easy, and friendly. Angel could see the servant warming to Allan's soft Southern tone.

'He is?' Gee said.

Allan nodded. 'I'm afraid so, Banner. We've got to find him or some bad men may hurt him. You wouldn't want that to happen, would you?'

The servant shook his head vigorously. 'No, suh, I sho' wouldn't.'

'Well, then. . . ?'

'He's gone to Daranga, see them gen'l'men there,' the man said. It was as if he was relieved to tell them.

'Birch and Reynolds?'

'That's right, suh.'

'That's fine, Banner,' Allan said, gently. 'I'll tell you what I'm going to do: to make sure you are safe, I'm goin' to leave a couple o' my men here with you. Then if the bad men come here looking for the senator, they'll be waiting.'

The Negro servant nodded eagerly. Allan looked at one of the men, who nodded.

They needed no words. Angel knew that the senator's house

would be thoroughly and carefully searched.

'Let's go,' he said. 'I have one more thing to do before I head for Daranga.'

'You're going back there?' Allan said. 'Maybe I'd better come with you.'

'Let's get down to River Road,.' Angel said. 'We can talk about that later.'

On the way down to the red light district he told the Marshal what his plan was. Allan nodded. Angel warmed again to this capable peace officer. He needed no long-winded explanations, but acted quickly and decisively. When they reached the house with the red roof, Angel crossed the street alone and went over to the door, lifting the heavy brass knocker and letting it fall until a lookout door popped open and a white face peered through it at him.

'Willy Mill sent me,' he said urgently. 'Open up.'

'We ain't – we're not open yet,' the woman said. 'Come back later.'

'I want to see Angela,' Angel rasped. 'And I want to see her now. Do I have to go and talk to the senator?'

The pale eyes widened in the white face and Angel heard the woman fumbling with a bolt.

'You'd better come in,' she mumbled. 'I'll go an' see . . .'

She was a thin, slatternly woman of about thirty, the dirty history of her life etched in the lines about the deep shadowed eyes. She had on a thin dress which barely concealed her body. The woman went up the stairs after showing Angel into a kind of salon, a parlor full of overstuffed furniture and heavy, dark wallpaper. The smell of cigar smoke and liquor and cheap perfume hung in the air. After a wait of perhaps five minutes Angel heard the swish of material and turned to see a tall woman, her face high-cheekboned and almost beautiful, hair tied tightly back, fine green eyes regarding his disheveled appearance with disdain. The dress of watered green silk was in the latest Eastern fashion. All in all Angela, for it was she, was a handsome woman and knew it.

'If Willy Mill sent you,' she said haughtily, 'he would also

140

have told you that we do not . . . entertain before ten o'clock.'

'Lady,' Angel said. 'You have a girl here named Kate Perry. Go and get her.'

The patrician eyebrows rose.

'I am not accustomed to being spoken to like that,' she said.

'Get used to it,' Angel snapped. 'It's polite compared to the way they talk in Yuma.'

For a moment she puzzled over his allusion, and then her brow cleared.

'Are you some kind of law officer?' she asked.

'You might say,' Angel told her. 'Get the girl.'

'You are making a mistake, my friend,' the woman said, ominously. 'I have connections in this town.'

'Not any more you haven't,' he said. 'If you mean the senator.'

She looked at him for a long, long moment, and then turned on her heel.

'Wait,' she said.

'Uh-huh,' Angel told her. 'Send someone for the girl. You stay here.'

Her eyes were fiery, but she came back into the room and pulled a cord hanging in the corner.

'You will regret this,' she hissed.

'I doubt it,' he said. The slatternly woman came in and Angela told her to fetch Kate Perry. 'The one in number eight,' was how she put it.

When they brought the girl in Angel felt his guts turn over in pure anger. She walked like a whipped animal, her head down, her long hair hanging over her face. Every inch of her seemed to cringe, as if her soul was buried in shame.

'Kate,' Angel said. She looked up at him and her eyes filled with huge tears. She gave a choking sob and hurled herself into his arms.

'Ohmygod,' she sobbed, 'Ohmygod!'

'It's all right now, Kate,' Angel said, clumsily. 'It's all right.' He smoothed her hair awkwardly with his hand. 'I've come to take you home.'

The girl sobbed uncontrollably and Angel patted her shoulder, looking up into the hate-filled eyes of the madam. She had a little derringer in her hand. The bore looked as big as a cannon and it was pointed right at Angel's head.

'Stand still,' Angela hissed. 'Very, very still. I think the senator will want to know you are here.'

'He's gone, Angela,' Angel said, pushing Kate Perry gently away from him. 'He's not at the hacienda.' Kate stood watching the exchange, her eyes wide.

'You're bluffing,' the madam said. 'He'll come.'

'No chance,' Angel told her. 'Put up the gun, Angela. Don't make things any worse than they are. You're already mixed up in a conspiracy to kidnap charge, not to mention some other things a good prosecutor might dream up if he was pushed to it.'

'You—' she rasped. 'Who else knows you're here?'

'I do,' said Allan. He had come in behind her, soundlessly, having entered the house from the rear. He tapped her neatly behind the ear with the barrel of his sixgun. Angela folded like a fan and the silk dress spread out like a pool of water as she slumped to the ground.

'Hate to do that to a woman,' Allan said. There wasn't an ounce of regret in his voice.

Kate Perry started to cry. The tears simply trickled hugely from her eyes. She made no sound, no sob. Her eyes simply welled with water, which trickled down her face and fell with soft thumps upon the carpeted floor.

'It's all right, Miss Perry,' Allan told her. 'It's all over.'

She shook her head, the tears raining down.

'I'll take her home with me,' Allan told Angel. 'My wife can get her some decent clothes. I'll have the doctor look in. She'll be all right, Angel.'

Angel nodded. 'Kate?' The girl looked at him. Her eyes shone with the tears she was trying desperately to hold back.

'Kate, I have to go now. I have to go to Daranga. You know why, don't you?'

The girl nodded again. The tears began once more.

'Don't cry,' Angel said. 'Go with Marshal Allan. When it's over I'll come back and take you home.'

'Yes,' she managed. 'Yes.'

Angel turned towards the door.

'Angel!' Allan called after him. 'You'll need horses!'

Angel grinned. 'I know just where I can get them, too,' he said. Then he was gone out into the night. Allan stood for a moment, his arm around the shoulders of the weeping girl.

'That's quite a man,' he said, almost to himself.

Kate Perry looked up at him and for the first time since he had seen her she smiled. 'Yes,' she said.

Angel sprinted up the street to the livery stable he had visited before. The same man sat on the same keg. It might even have been the same bottle of beer. He looked at Angel, his mouth a surprised 'O'.

'Howdy,' Angel nodded. 'How many horses you got in?'

'Uh . . . er . . . I . . . six . . . six – mebbe seven,' the man stuttered. 'Why'd you ask?'

'Just wondering,' Angel said. 'Any really fine horses?'

'Couple,' the man said, wonderingly. 'Whuffor?'

'They'd be the senator's, I guess,' Angel went on. The man nodded.

'Good stock they are,' he said, proudly. 'Palominos.'

'Incredible,' Angel said, and his voice changed suddenly. 'Saddle them.'

'Saddle 'em?' squeaked the man, almost swallowing his Adam's apple.

'Quick,' Angel said. The hostler looked down to see the sixgun jamming into his belly. He gulped another gigantic swallow, down and bobbed his head.

'Uh . . . now . . . see here, mister . . .'

'Move!'

Angel stood over the man as he saddled the two horses. They were superb animals: they had the fine deep chests and long muscles of racehorses and Angel felt a fleeting sadness at what he was going to have to do to them.

'Mister,' wheedled the hostler, 'the senator's goin' to have my cojones on his watch-chain when he finds out what's happened. I hate to think what he's goin' to do to you, but it'll shore be unpleasant.'

Angel looked at the man for a long moment, frowning.

'Knew there was something,' he said finally.

He laid the barrel of his sixgun along the side of the man's head, dropping him like a sack in the dust. He picked up the beer bottle and emptied the contents down his throat, remembering that he hadn't eaten. The stars were out in splendor as he gigged the spirited horses towards the edge of town. He paused for a moment to look up at the sky. Then he took a deep breath and kicked the startled horses into a thundering gallop.

CHAPTER TWENTY-FOUR

Larkin came down Fort Street.

His clothes were white with trail dust and his eyes peered from an alkali mask. They burned with a lambent fire that bordered on madness. He had ridden in a huge half circle, out to the Reynolds ranch and then on to the Birch place, scouting each of them like an Indian, waiting until he could get near the main buildings and see either of the two men whose names he kept repeating to himself like a litany. Neither had been there, so he knew now that they were in town and he was coming in to get them and nothing, nothing was going to stop him. He had slept fitfully in a small stand of ironwood trees in the Rio Blanco valley, twitching as he slept, his lips making small sounds. At dawn he had saddled his horse again and now, as the sun climbed the far side of the sky, he was at Daranga. He watched the people on the sidewalks with hating eyes, and they saw him and the word ran alongside and ahead of him. He came down Fort Street and Sunny Metter stepped out into the street, a carbine in his hands.

'Larkin!' he shouted.

Larkin shot him down. Nobody saw him move. Metter didn't even have a chance to fire. One second Larkin was motionless, the next Metter had been blasted backwards, his hands clutching at the dust, blood welling from his right shoulder, knees drawn up in agony. Larkin kneed the horse on, ignoring the Mexican girl who ran out to where Metter lay.

'*Sinverguenza!*' she spat. '*Hijo de la gran puta!*'

'Ma'am,' Larkin acknowledged, touching his hat. He felt good. All his sinews were loose and the old fire was racing in his veins. He wondered for a brief moment why the man had tried to stop him but then dismissed the thought. It didn't matter. He dismounted outside the Alhambra and pushed in through the swinging doors.

The Alhambra was by any standards a very fancy saloon. The long bar curved around the room in a horseshoe, gleaming black mahogany polished to a high shine. Behind it, fancy fretted woodwork shelves backed with cut glass mirrors reflected the amber gleam of dozens of neatly arranged bottles. The floor was smooth-planed pine, scattered with sawdust. Brass spittoons punctuated the brass footrail every three or four feet. To one side of the room there were tables, several set up for gambling: poker, blackjack, faro, chuckaluck. A stairway led to a balcony which ran around the room like a minstrel gallery, with doors leading off that were occupied by the girls who worked in the place. Larkin saw all this in one swift glance, and in the same glance he saw Birch sitting at a table with Burnstine. The place was almost empty. A swamper looked up and saw Larkin in the doorway, and almost fell over himself getting out of the way. His pail rattled and the two men looked up and saw Larkin there.

Burnstine's eyes widened with fear, but Birch betrayed no emotion at all. He merely stared at the gunman, his eyes opaque.

'Well, well,' Larkin said. 'Two birds with one stone.'

'What do you want, Larkin?' Birch said, his voice hard.

'You, you bastard!' Larkin spat. 'You an' Reynolds set me up. I played it straight and you set me up.'

A man ran from the room. The others cowered back against the bar as far away from the probable line of fire as they could get. No one moved a muscle. The air was charged with menace.

'Don't be a fool, Larkin!' Birch rasped. 'Try that here and you're a dead man.'

'Sure,' Larkin said, his voice soft and easy. He directed his gaze at the cowering Burnstine. 'Stand up, Senator!'

Burnstine looked at Birch. The big man nodded and they stood up together, chairs scraping on the floor. Birch moved off to one side away from the politician. Larkin watched them like a cat.

'I'm not armed,' Burnstine stammered. 'It'll be cold-blooded murder, Larkin!'

'It don't bother me none,' Larkin informed him. So intent upon the two men was his gaze that he did not hear the door open soundlessly on the balcony above him, but Birch did. From beneath his jutting eyebrows he saw the slim figure of Jacey Reynolds, gun in hand, move to the rail of the balcony.

'I don't care much which o' you goes first,' Larkin said. He might have been discussing the weather.

Up on the balcony, Reynolds leaned over and cocked the gun and fired but Larkin, his reflexes honed to razor sharpness, heard the sound of the ratchet and was moving. He threw himself backwards and to one side, firing at the man on the balcony. Reynolds grunted as the slug smashed through him and then teetered for a moment, tipping forward, folding across the rail, somersaulting down to the bar, smashing flat on the polished mahogany counter even as Larkin went on with his roll, trying for the shelter of one of the tables. Birch had a second's advantage and that was enough. His gun was out and spouting fire, three shots in a rising arc as the gunman scrambled across the floor. Birch's first shot smashed Larkin's right hand to a mangled mess of muscle and white bone. The second one hit him almost in the middle of the chest, slam-

146

ming Larkin flat on the floor. The third, slightly wild, hit Larkin's left thigh. He lay there on the sawdusted floor, and Birch stalked over to him, cocking the gun again.

'So long, Larkin,' he said callously and raised the gun. Larkin looked up and tried to spit at the rancher towering above him. Every eye in the place was fixed on the pair. Nobody saw Angel come in.

'Birch!' he shouted.

Every head turned. They saw Angel standing there and they saw that his gun was not drawn. Birch, too, turned half around, crouched like a cat ready to spring, the leveled gun in his hand cocked and ready to fire.

'It's Angel!' Burnstine shouted.

A look of purest animal joy flitted across Birch's face: the thoughts in his head were plain to everyone watching. Birch whipped the gun around. What happened next became a legend in Daranga. Newcomers would be told the story, and they would shake their head in disbelief and say it couldn't be done, but the men in the Alhambra saw it done and terrible though it was, it was magnificent. In the same fraction of time that the big man moved, Angel also moved, his hand sweeping up in a motion too fast for the eye to follow, the sixgun blasting flame once, twice, three times as Birch's gun exploded harmlessly into the ground, the big man dead as he fired. Birch's death was so shocking, so impossible, that when he fell there was a silence of stunning intensity. The big man lay on his back. There were two neat holes just above the third button of his dark blue shirt, and another had been drilled dead center between the opaque eyes. Angel stood half crouched, his grey eyes still cold and deadly.

'You?' Burnstine managed. His face held the expression of a man witnessing the end of the world. Angel said nothing. He looked at Burnstine and the senator saw Angel's trigger finger whiten. Burnstine looked into the cold and grinning skull face of death and his jaw slackened.

'God, don't, Angel!' he cried hoarsely. 'You've got to give me justice!'

The last word seemed to release a hidden switch in Angel. The watchers saw the man slowly straighten, slightly, easily letting the tension slip away. Angel sighed, the barrel of the gun dropping slightly. And Burnstine knew he would live. He was soaking wet with the sallow sweat of terror. At that moment Sheriff Austin burst into the room, closely followed by two soldiers. Angel whirled to meet the new threat, the sixgun level and the killing readiness back in his eyes.

'Christ, Angel!' screeched Austin. 'It's me!'

His discomfiture was so profound that it almost totally dissipated the tension in the big room. Even Angel gave a tired grin.

'For a moment, there, Sheriff, I thought it was a man,' he said.

'What in the name o' God's been goin' on?' stuttered Austin. His eyes fell on the bodies. 'Birch? Reynolds! What in the name of sweet Jesus. . . ?' Larkin groaned. He lay in a widening pool of blood, but his eyes flickered open and he looked around.

'That bastard!' Austin said. 'He shot Sunny Metter, you know that, Angel?'

'I saw it happen,' Angel said. 'I was too far away to do anything about it.

'Why did he try to take Larkin? He should have known he couldn't do it.'

'He can tell you that hisself,' Austin blustered. 'He ain't hurt bad.' Angel felt a warm flooding feeling of relief at this news. 'I'll go see him,' he said. 'Sheriff, this here is Senator Ludlow Burnstine. Lock him up.'

Austin had started forward, his hand extended. At Angel's words he stopped, his jaw dropping comically.

'Lock him? *Up?*' he strangled out.

'Tight,' emphasized Angel. 'Two guards outside his door.'

Austin gulped. 'You can't lock up no United States senator, Angel!' he yelped.

'Oh, shut up and do what I tell you, man!' snapped Angel. 'He won't give you no argument. He's plain glad to be alive.'

He motioned to one of the soldiers. 'Give me a hand with Larkin,' he said.

They lifted the gunman up, and Larkin shouted something from the depths of his pain as they moved him. He was quite unconscious by the time they got him to the hotel and sent for the doctor. The doctor opened his bag, snipping Larkin's shirt away and probing gently at the wound in his chest with his fingers. He rose and snapped his bag shut. Angel watched him expressionlessly.

'He might hang on another twenty-four hours,' the doctor said. 'I can't do anything for him. Patch him up, maybe I'll send my wife across to bandage him up, make him a little more comfortable. I'll look in this evening.'

As quickly as he had come, the old doctor was gone. Angel stood alone in the room watching the unconscious man. After a while, he left.

CHAPTER
TWENTY-FIVE

Later in the day, after a huge meal and a bath and shave, fresh clothes on his back and a feeling of well-being in his soul, Angel sat in the upstairs room with Sunny Metter and Lieutenant Blackstone.

'Looks like you tied it all up, Frank,' Metter said, weakly. He cursed as a movement brought a stabbing pain through his shoulder.

Angel shook his head. 'If you aren't the world's fattest fool,' he said pityingly. 'What in the name of God made you try to stop Larkin?'

'I don't honestly know,' Metter admitted ruefully. 'I figger'd he'd give the soldiers the slip, maybe head for the Reynolds place, then Birch's. If he found out they weren't there, I guessed he'd come to Daranga, so I made tracks here. I guess what was goin' on in my head was that if he got to Birch an' Reynolds, your case would go up in smoke. I didn't know about Burnstine, of course. It just come into my head to try an' stop him. Damnfool thing to do, no?'

The soldier nodded, grinning, and Angel smiled, too.

'How is Larkin?' Blackstone asked. Angel shook his head. 'Doc says he won't make it.'

'Good riddance,' snapped Blackstone. 'Did he tell you anything?'

'Nothing,' Angel told them. 'I went over to see him just a while ago.' He had been told that Larkin was conscious and wanted to talk to him. The gunman had been sitting propped up in the bed, his face chalky beneath the tan, his eyes receded deep into the skull. He smiled weakly, eyes unreadable.

'I reckon I owe you somethin',' he said softly.

'Not a thing,' Angel had said. 'It just broke that way.'

'Never figured on Reynolds at all,' Larkin said. 'I must be gettin' soft.'

He saw the expression on Angel's face and his smile faded.

'Give it to me straight, Angel,' he whispered. 'Ain't goin' to pull through this time, am I?'

'No,' Angel said.

Larkin sighed. 'Pity,' he said. 'I had a lot o' things I wanted to do.'

'You could go out clean,' Angel suggested.

'Spill, you mean?' Larkin shook his head. 'Not my style, Angel.' There was real regret in his voice. 'I'd like to pay up what I owe you. But not that. Besides, who'd believe the word of a hired gun?'

'I would,' Angel told him levelly.

'I'm thankin' you for that,' Larkin said gratefully. 'But it's no go, man. I allus went by my own rules.'

'Pity,' Angel said. 'It would nail Burnstine good. He'd hang, Larkin.'

'Hangin's too good for that bastard,' spat Larkin. He coughed, and bloody flecks of foam speckled his bloodless lips.

After a moment, he asked a question.

'Metter's just fine,' Angel told him. 'It was just a flesh wound.'

Larkin nodded. 'That's how I shot it,' he said, and Angel detected a curious sort of pride in the man's voice, as though it was important that he should believe that Larkin had known exactly where the bullet that had felled Metter would hit.

'You sure, Larkin?' Angel tried one last time. 'It'd be nice to go with your head high.'

'I'll do that,' Larkin had said. 'Don't you worry.'

Angel had left him then; the gunman had been staring up at the ceiling, his eyes empty and his mouth tight in a thin grimace of pain when he closed the door.

'Hard as nails,' Blackstone said, whistling through his teeth at the end of Angel's recital. 'Right to the end.'

Metter changed the subject. 'How did Thompson take the news?' he wanted to know.

'Pretty badly,' the young lieutenant said. 'He headed back to the Fort with Sergeant Battle. It was like talking to someone who was already dead.'

'Does he know enough to help you, Frank?' asked Metter.

'Some,' Angel said. 'It's hard to say whether it will be enough.'

'But you doubt it,' Metter insisted.

'There'll be enough to send the old man to jail for years,' Angel said. 'He's finished, sure enough.'

'But Perry, and Clare . . . all those men at the high chaparral ranches,' Blackstone put in. 'You mean he could get away with that?'

'He could,' Angel admitted. 'With Birch and Reynolds dead, Boot and Mill gone, we don't have evidence of his involvement. Not tangible evidence, anyway, although there's enough circumstantial evidence to hang him ten times over.'

'Frank, you've done all you can,' Metter said, sympathetically. 'Don't knock yourself out because you couldn't get a full house.'

Angel got up from his chair.

'I think I'll have a talk with the senator one last time,' he said.

He went downstairs to the bar, where Burnstine sat patiently in a chair, his composure intact, fully in control of himself

151

again. Burnstine's fertile mind had been working like a well-oiled machine, checking this facet of his involvement in the Rio Blanco troubles against that. Nothing had ever been put in writing which could connect him with Larkin, with Boot, with Mill. Witnesses might be found who could testify that they had been seen visiting his house, but that could easily have been innocent. Alternatively, witnesses could become uncertain if pressures were applied. There were still plenty of strings he could pull which these fools knew nothing about. His ownership through mortgages of the Rio Blanco ranches was pure business, nothing more. How was he to know that Birch and Reynolds had been crooks? They had paid up on the dot the monies due him each month, and he could certainly prove that. His bookkeeping was impeccable, for Burnstine knew that accounts which had no flaws in them were often considered the hallmark of an honest man, and he had employed one of the best accountants in the Territory to work on his books, all honest and above board. No, he was safe. There might be all sorts of accusations, but none of them would stick. With the conclusion of these thoughts he had politely asked one of the guards if he might have a drink. It was rotgut brandy, of course, but better than nothing. He still had a few cigars. He was sitting now behind a baize-covered table in the saloon, expansive in the bentwood chair, cigar alight, brandy warming in his hand. Angel came down the stairs.

'My dear Angel,' Burnstine smiled a welcome. 'Won't you join me?'

Angel looked at the politician for a moment, and then with a contemptuous sweep of his arm, knocked the liquor off the table, the glass smashing to fragments against the bar. Then he leaned over and plucked the cigar from Burnstine's mouth and tossed it away. Burnstine looked at Angel and there was complete and seething hatred in his eyes.

'Damn you, Angel,' he said, his voice low-pitched and cold.

'Murderers don't get treated like kings by me,' Angel told him, his contempt lashing the vanity of the old man. Burnstine half rose to his feet and then a slow smile touched his face. He leaned back in the chair.

'You're a fool, Angel,' he said. 'I thought you were an intel-ligent man, but I see now that you are just muscle, Larkin's kind, only on the side of law and order. You are not worth wast-ing time on.'

'Senator, I am going to see you hanged,' Angel promised him, levelly.

'On what charge, may I ask?' Burnstine asked. He was begin-ning to enjoy himself. He had gone over and over everything in his mind. He was safe and inside he felt the warm glow the knowledge created. What could this ... this hireling do to him? 'Who will bring evidence, may I ask?' he continued. 'Birch? Dead. Reynolds? Dead. Boot and Mill, I assume by your continued existence, dead. Larkin? Dead in all but fact, so my guards tell me. You have been far too efficient in your narrow way, Angel. You have not brought me down as you so fondly hoped: you have in fact ensured my survival. Oh, I agree: a little dirt may stick, it always does. I'll simply say that it's politi-cal jealousy in Washington, something trumped-up to discredit me, the way things are always trumped up against successful people. My scheme will go through, Angel, and there's noth-ing you can do to stop it.' He sat back, smiling.

'I could kill you myself,' Angel said, reflectively. He put no emphasis on the words, and Burnstine paled. Then anger mottled his face and he jabbed a finger forward.

'You!' he hissed. 'You will be the one who dies, Angel!' The charming façade slipped away from the benign politician's face, and the sleeping tiger beneath it appeared. The hate-filled eyes smouldered, the megalomaniac who had planned this gigantic plot, the real Burnstine, the calculating, cold-blooded manipulator who had brought the reign of terror and destruction down upon the Rio Blanco valley, showed in every straining fiber of the man's body. The man was evil incarnate and despite himself, Angel recoiled slightly from the venomous power of the man, a thing almost tangible.

'You, Angel, will be lucky if you reach Washington alive,' Burnstine hissed. 'I will put out word on you. Wherever you go, whatever you do, someone I have sent will be close behind you, dogging your footsteps. If I have to spend a million dollars – and I can, Angel, I can – I will have you dead! Somewhere, sometime, they will find you. You may stop one of them, or even two. You may hide in the remotest part of the world. But someone will find you. Waking, sleeping, wherever you are, however long it may take, they will find you and kill you. Now get away from me. I'm sick of the sight of your face!'

The hard and certain power of the old man's words touched a chill finger on Angel's spine. He felt doubt seep into his mind: he knew Washington, knew the endless years that Burnstine could, and would, fight through the courts, his case shuttled from committee to sub-committee, the buck always passing on. Few men in the capital would want to have the black mark on their political career that condemning a senator of the United States Government to death would make. No matter the justice of it, the human rightness involved. This evil old man with his millions could stay his execution for a year, two, ten, and all of those years would be filled for Angel with the fear of the assassin in the night, the bullet from the darkened alley, somewhere, sometime, never knowing when. Angel got up out of the chair.

He went out of the room without speaking and he heard the old man laugh as he went, a sound like a snake in a basket full of newspapers.

CHAPTER
TWENTY-SIX

Nobody ever found out how Larkin did it.

It might have been that he spent his last dollars bribing one of the young soldiers who were guarding him, or he might even have somehow, in some incredible fashion, managed to get out of the hotel without being seen. It was late in the evening. Angel was upstairs with Metter and Blackstone, awaiting the arrival of the US marshal, and the saloon downstairs was dark except for a light on the table in front of Senator Burnstine, who was playing cards with the sheriff. Burnstine was in an expansive mood, losing large sums of money with a happy laugh, his belly warm with cheap brandy, a fine cigar smouldering in the ashtray. He dealt Austin five cards and was just about to deal himself a hand when he looked up. The cards slipped from his fingers as if they had turned to wax. His jaw gaped open and Austin, who was sitting with his back to the door, turned in his chair. His bowels turned to jelly. Framed in the doorway, a street window lighting him against the night darkness, stood Larkin. He was leaning against the door-jamb and they could hear him struggling to breathe. The sound was like an old, rusty pump being used for the first time in many years. Larkin lurched into the saloon, standing about six feet away from them, just inside the circle of lamplight. Austin gasped when he saw the front of the man's body: it was a pulsing mass of thick, black blood. Larkin was all but dead on his feet, his wound torn open by the terrible effort of getting from the hotel to Metter's place. But the eyes held that burning, blank, killing light that Austin had seen before and he sat frozen in the chair, his tongue paralyzed in his mouth.

'Senator,' Larkin said. He lifted his bandaged right hand a few inches in greeting and they saw that the white linen was also bright red with blood.

'How in the name of God. . . ?' Austin finally managed.

'Don' know,' Larkin said. 'Leg's like pulp. Just about made it.' He grinned, pain drawing his face into a terrible death's head. 'Couldn't go 'thout sayin' bye, could I?' His voice slurred.

He let them see the sixgun and Burnstine's eyes touched it and then rolled up in his head. 'Oh God,' he said.

'No help comin' from that quarter, Burnstine,' sneered Larkin. He lurched, almost falling. Then he drew himself upright. His willpower was astonishing. Burnstine scrabbled out of his chair, fell to his knees, crawling towards Larkin.

'Don't,' he sobbed, 'don't, don't, don't. I'll do anything. Only don't. . . .' He was abject, craven; nothing in him left functioning. The pungent smell of sweat and urine arose from him and Austin's nostrils wrinkled in distaste and horror. The man had come apart.

'I – uh – Larkin. . . .' he began, trying to find courage to tell Larkin that he was going to shout for help, but the words just would not come. Austin stared at Larkin in fascinated horror, totally terrified, completely prevented by the sight of the man from intervening in what was happening.

Burnstine sobbed and crawled across the floor towards Larkin.

'Get up, Senator,' Larkin said, softly, his voice fading away. His eyes closed for a second, then jerked open again. 'Get up. I'm not going to kill you. It's all right. Get up.'

Burnstine looked up from the floor, hope kindling in his eyes, his face red raw with tears of terror, his nose dribbling, his mouth wet and loose. He looked at Larkin to see if this was some terrible, final jest and Larkin said again, 'Get up, Senator. Get up.'

Burnstine got to his feet, babbling, his hands moving like butterflies on pins.

'You'll never regret it, Larkin, David, my boy,' he sobbed. 'I'll give you money, anything, anything you want. Just tell me . . . tell me.'

'Sit down, Senator,' Larkin said. His voice sounded very far away. 'Don't be afraid. It's all right.'

Burnstine fell into the chair, knuckling the tears and snot off his face, his eyes touching Austin with something like a plea, and he let his shoulders relax, a hiccup shaking his body.

'You . . . won't. . . ?' he tremulously began. Larkin shook his head and for the first time, a spark came back into Burnstine's eyes, the thinnest edge of the foxy craftiness, the first faint sign that the brain was beginning to function, to emerge from its deep black plummet into terror. Austin saw Burnstine's eyes flick over the swaying Larkin, calculating how long, how much longer the dying man could stand.

'That's my senator,' said Larkin and shot Burnstine in the face three times. The shocking sound of the sixgun, the flash of the powder by his face made Austin scream with pure terror and he had fainted dead away when Angel came down the stairs three at a time, Blackstone behind him.

Blackstone went quickly to Burnstine's side. He recoiled at the sight of the old man's head. Austin sat up, then keeled over to one side, vomiting. His face had been resting in Burnstine's bloody brains.

Angel kneeled by Larkin's side. The gunman coughed, and a gobbet of blood coursed down his chin. His eyes looked up into Angel's and he suddenly smiled, a bright, happy child's smile.

'Now we're even,' he said. And then he died. Angel never knew whether Larkin meant himself and Burnstine, or himself and Angel. Much later he would realize that Larkin had meant both.

CHAPTER TWENTY-SEVEN

The Palace Hotel in San Francisco was one of the finest in America. Renowned for its cuisine, for its palatial luxury, the Palace attracted the most handsome men and the most beautiful women in the world to its portals. At this time of year it was crowded with the rich, the famous, and the hungry swirling motley multitude of seekers for fame and fortune who came to California like a never-ending torrent.

Frank Angel sat in the dining room, looking at Kate Perry across the snowy expanse of linen and gleaming silver on their table. He raised his wine glass and made a silent toast to her. She smiled back.

It had been two weeks since that last fateful night in Daranga. With the death of Burnstine, the troubles in the Rio Blanco valley had come to a bloody and sudden end. There had been reports to send to Washington, and many loose ends to tie up. But that was all behind them now. Kate Perry was a very rich young woman, for the Government purchase of the portion of the ranches which were to be flooded, both her father's and Walt Clare's, would be a generous one, all of it hers by unarguable right. Even now, Army engineers were surveying the canyon of the Rio Blanco, and the booming dynamite could be clearly heard in Daranga. Angel had bidden his friends a last goodbye and then they had been free to go. They had been driven in an Army ambulance, with an escort headed by Lieutenant Blackstone and proudly led by Sergeant Battle, across to Tucson and from there they had come to San Francisco. The sweeping bay with its happily-named islands had enchanted them, and the blush of roses had softly come again to Kate Perry's cheeks. She had gone shopping in the busy streets with a childlike abandon, and the pale blue dress she had bought brought out the beauty that rough clothes had only hinted at.

Still, what she had gone through had scarred her deeply, and for a while she had flinched whenever Angel touched her hand, her arm. Then, one night, her mood had changed, and the girl had become a woman. Afterwards, in the big, high-ceilinged room with the plaster cupids in the corners, she had cried for a long time, finally falling asleep in his arms. He had lain awake long into the night, watching her sleeping. What Kate Perry had lived through, survived, would have broken most women. Her courage was something he could under-stand and admire, and he knew that now she was whole again, what had been between them would change. He had felt the old restlessness, too. Now they sat, warmth between them and sadness as well, and she said softly:

'You want to go.'

'I'll be around for a while,' he told her.

'Only . . . a while, Frank?'

He looked out of the window and watched the clanging, noisy bustle in the streets of San Francisco.

'I have money, Frank,' she said softly, as if reading his thoughts. 'I . . . we could go anywhere. Anywhere you wanted to. . . .'

'I know,' he said softly. 'But it's not for me. I have my work.'

'Your work?' she said, surprise in her voice. 'Your work?'

'It's what I do,' he said doggedly. 'What I am.'

She fell silent for a long, long moment, toying with the knife beside her plate. 'You will not be tied down, is that it?'

'I guess so,' Angel said. He was uncomfortable, talking about it. 'I can't live steady, Kate. I need the change, and the challenge. Living the same life day after day after day – that would be a sort of death for me.'

'We could be happy, together,' she reminded him. 'We are. Happy. And safe.'

'Safe?' he echoed. 'I don't want safety, Kate. Being safe is like saying you're just waiting to die.'

'This job,' she managed at last. 'Somewhere, one day, you will die. Someone will kill you. You know that.'

'All the more reason to live,' he said. 'Really live now. Not just exist.'

She looked at him again and he looked at her, and they got up and went out of the dining-room, the surprised head waiter watching them go with raised eyebrows, then nodding wisely, These honeymooners, he thought. He had seen thousands in his time. They always made him sentimental. He would buy Rosa some flowers tonight, he thought.

In the big room Kate Perry came into Angel's arms all golden and warm and in her love for him and his for her, they found all the giving that could be done. Tomorrow, she would lose him. Tomorrow, he would go out of her life and back to that other, harder, deadlier life to which he truly belonged.

'But that's tomorrow,' she said softly and blew out the light.